THE

EMPIRE

of

DIRT

THE

FRANCESCA

EMPIRE

MANFREDI

OF DIRT

A Novel | Translated by Ekin Oklap

W. W. NORTON & COMPANY
Independent Publishers Since 1923

For information about permission to reproduce selections from this book, write to Permissions, W. W. Norton & Company, Inc., 500 Fifth Avenue, New York, NY 10110

For information about special discounts for bulk purchases, please contact W. W. Norton Special Sales at specialsales@wwnorton.com or 800-233-4830

Manufacturing by Lakeside Book Company
Book design by Beth Steidle
Production manager: Beth Steidle

Library of Congress Cataloging-in-Publication Data

Names: Manfredi, Francesca, 1988– author. | Oklap, Ekin, translator.
Title: The empire of dirt : a novel / Francesca Manfredi ; translated by Ekin Oklap.
Other titles: Impero della polvere. English
Description: New York, NY : W. W. Norton & Company, Inc., [2022] |
Originally published in Italian as L'impero della polvere.
Identifiers: LCCN 2022009040 | ISBN 9780393881776 (paperback) | ISBN 9780393881783 (epub)
Subjects: LCGFT: Domestic fiction. | Paranormal fiction. | Novels.
Classification: LCC PQ4913.A68214 I4713 2022 | DDC 853/.92—dc23/eng/20220222
LC record available at https://lccn.loc.gov/2022009040

W. W. Norton & Company, Inc., 500 Fifth Avenue, New York, N.Y. 10110
www.wwnorton.com

W. W. Norton & Company Ltd., 15 Carlisle Street, London W1D 3BS

1 2 3 4 5 6 7 8 9 0

And you could have it all
My empire of dirt
I will let you down
I will make you hurt.

TRENT REZNOR,
"Hurt"

Women are like that they don't
acquire knowledge of people we
are for that they are just born
with a practical fertility of suspi-
cion that makes a crop every so
often and usually right they have
an affinity for evil for supplying
whatever the evil lacks in itself for
drawing it about them instinctively
as you do bed-clothing in slumber
fertilising the mind for it until the
evil has served its purpose whether
it ever existed or no.

WILLIAM FAULKNER,
The Sound and the Fury

CONTENTS

THE

EMPIRE

of

DIRT

PROLOGUE

THE FIRST TIME I ASKED MY GRANDMOTHER A QUES-
tion like that, I was six years old. I remember the moment well,
and I think she would remember it too, if she could. I asked
her where the stomachache that tormented her every day had
come from. Back then I would sometimes see her standing in
the kitchen or in the hallway, massaging her belly when she
thought no one was looking. She never did it in front of us.
She would find a space, a moment for herself when she could

yield to what I later learned were stabbing pains, sharp and persistent—if not as strong as those that ended up taking her from us.

That day I found her leaning against the kitchen counter. The stove was on, and she had one hand on the countertop beside it, the other resting just beneath her navel. She was rubbing circles over her stomach and pressing hard, like when you have a stain on your dress and you're trying to get it out. Her eyes were closed, and I couldn't see what expression they carried because she noticed my presence almost immediately, straightening up and letting her arms fall to her sides.

That was when I asked her about it. It was a naïve question, the kind a little girl would ask, the kind of question adults will respond to in a rational way, splintering the place they come from—a place where logic and physics don't yet apply, and where different things happen for different reasons every time, influenced at times by chance and at other times by magic. It was the kind of question to which I was sure my grandmother would respond firmly, precisely, and reassuringly. Or perhaps she would bring out one of those sharp and well-honed remarks she deployed whenever anyone stepped over the line and needed putting back in their place. Why don't you mind your own business? she would say. There are some things you oughtn't ask about. We must have given you too big a mouth. Come here, let me have a look. She would have stood there staring at me through narrowed eyes, her eyebrows raised into an arch. Then she would have laughed. It was her way of defending what was hers, of keeping in check anyone who tried to venture into her private world. She belonged to a different era and never tired of teaching good manners; she considered them to be the most effective line of defense against unwelcome intrusions, and most of the time, she was right.

But that day all she did was look at me. She picked out one of her long, thin cigarettes from the pack she kept in the pocket of her apron, and lit it with a match. She took a deep drag, then blew the smoke out in a tidy plume. There is a limit, she said, there is a limit to what we are able to carry inside. It might go and curl up in some quiet corner at first. We all have our places, she said. It might hide in there for a while, not bothering anyone, but one day it will decide the time has come to remind you that it is still there, that it is vast, and after that you will never be able to forget again.

That is how we are made. It is as God wills it, she said, placing her hand back on her stomach. Once it learns how to fill up, it will never stay empty for long. Your mother was inside here once. That is where I still feel her, every time anything bad happens.

ONE

IT CAME SILENTLY, STEALTHILY. IT CAME AT NIGHT, when all terrible things happen, and like all terrible things, it decided to give me a choice. It was thin and slippery; it was hot and seductive, like a voice inviting you to do something you shouldn't. It was irrevocably there, yet it also seemed to say that if I wanted to, if I was clever enough not to tell anyone about it, I could leave it right where I'd found it, in that bathroom that night. I could choose to get up, close the door, and go back to sleep, and nothing would change.

What I did not know then is that you can't hide something like that for long. You can choose to keep it sealed away, but you cannot prevent it from growing. And like all liquids, the tighter you compress it, the more it will seethe, until one day it will burst out with the force of a thunderstorm.

But I was twelve years old, and no one had ever explained to me what was going to happen. Even if they had, it would have made no difference that night. These are things you learn much later on, and always at your own expense.

I chose to listen to the voice, and kept the secret.

HOUSE

PEOPLE IN TOWN USED TO CALL IT "THE BLIND
house" because only three of the walls had windows, and even
those were tiny, and the wall that greeted those who came
up from the road had none at all. From that angle the house
looked like a block of white concrete, a shoebox. I would hear
the older boys sometimes, during recess at school: "That's the
girl who lives in the blind house."

After what happened in 1996, they started calling it "the black house" or "the cursed house" or even "the house with a thousand legs," after the dark bugs that could still be seen crawling over the white walls, according to those who dared get close enough to look. Few people used these names in front of me, and few people ever approached the house: just the postman, who came twice a week, and in the evenings, local kids egged on by their friends. They would come close enough to ring the bell, then run away as fast as they could, back onto the road that led to town. Eventually people lost interest in the house, and the events that had occurred there took on the contours of legend, a story that was told over and over, changing every time depending on who told it, until finally it became a distant episode, remote in time and space: something cold, dead, that need no longer be feared or summoned, and was overshadowed by the more sensational news stories appearing on television.

•

THE BLIND HOUSE: that's what my mother called it too, shaking her head and with her voice full of scorn every time something broke—a tap starting to drip only weeks after the plumber's last visit; a wooden shutter consumed by damp breaking in half when it was pulled shut a little too firmly. The blind house, she would repeat in a hard tone, as if it were a thing she could not break free of. My grandmother would pretend she couldn't hear her, or she would merely smile, but I knew that it affected her more than she was willing to show. The house had been built by her grandparents and by her parents before they'd even had her. She was born there, in one of the rooms on the second floor—she had never told us which one—and in there she had given birth to my mother, and to my aunts before her. The house was surrounded by fields, vegetable gardens, stables, and enclosures for the livestock. We had chickens, rabbits, ducks, goats, sheep, and cows, though their numbers had gradually diminished ever since my grandfather had died. When I was born, there were two horses and a donkey. When Grandma was little, there had been three horses and four donkeys. She said they had served to carry produce to town on market day, before there were vans or cars. We didn't have much use for the donkey anymore but we kept it because my mother liked it, and my grandmother had grown fond of it, too. Sometimes horses would mate with donkeys, producing a mule or a hinny. These animals are sterile but sturdy: we still had a mule now, the sole survivor from that earlier time of horses and donkeys. It had a disproportionately large head and sad eyes. When it raised its ears, it looked like a rabbit. When I was little I would ask to be lifted up onto its back, and I would pretend that I was riding a giant bunny.

The third and last floor of the house used to be a granary back in the day, or so my mother had told me. Before it became my room, it had been used as an attic. I have some memories, however foggy, of that old attic: an army of boxes, rusty bicycles and old toys, and an oblique, silty light filtering through windows darkened by years of dust and filth. The attic was where I went to hide every time I fought with my mother. I would emerge only when it was time for dinner, and go downstairs with my clothes covered in dust and my hands black. My grandmother would be waiting on the stairs to intercept me and take me to the bathroom, where she would pull my dress off over my head and scrub me with soap until—so she would say—I looked presentable for Mother. I must have been seven or eight when my mother decided to clear out the attic and turn it into my bedroom. I had long since stopped sleeping in my parents' room, and instead slept in my grandmother's room, across from theirs. My mother warned me that I would be moved to the attic only the day the work began. She woke me up on her way out of the house. My grandmother must have been downstairs or in the garden; she tended to wake up at dawn, especially in the summer, to make a start on the household chores before it got too hot. My mother slipped into the room and sat on the edge of the bed; she stroked my hair until I opened my eyes, then smiled at me.

"I was thinking you shouldn't sleep in here anymore," she said.

"Why?"

"Because you're a big girl now, and big girls should have their own rooms."

I thought of how the house didn't have any other rooms besides those we were already using. "Will I have to go to another house?" I said.

She smiled in that way she had, lifting only one corner of her mouth, and shook her head. "Which room do you like best?"

Then she kissed my forehead and left without waiting for an answer. The workmen arrived soon after that to clear out the dust-coated furniture and the boxes from the attic. They put them in a pile out in the courtyard while my grandmother and I looked on wordlessly. In the days that followed, my father laid newspaper over the floor and painted the room blue. He set up a desk, a wardrobe, a little bookcase, and a new bed, because the one I had been using in Grandma's room, and which had once belonged to my granddad, could not be carried up the stairs.

On my first night up there, my mother came in to wish me good night. The paper lampshade let through a thin light, which reflected off the sloping roof right in front of the bed, lengthening the shadows and making the furniture look longer, the ceiling taller.

"Why do I have to be up here?" I asked my mother as she tucked me in.

"I've left a surprise for you," she said. "You'll see when I turn the lights off. Good night, Valentina."

She stood up and clicked the switch off before walking out and leaving the door ajar. I saw then that the ceiling was decked with stars. Tiny, sticky stars that glowed yellow in the dark. I felt a hollowness in my chest and I began to cry, quietly, the tears rolling down my neck and wetting the pillow.

•

THE INTERIOR OF the house was made of wood, and at night, especially in the summer, the whole building creaked, as if there were some invisible creature stepping on the floors, or as if the house itself were complaining. When I was little, if I woke up in the middle of the night or had trouble falling asleep, I would tiptoe downstairs barefoot to call for my father, but no matter what he did to soothe me, no matter how many times he tried to explain that it was just the wood settling, adapting to the changes in temperature, alternately expanding and contracting, I never stopped reading in those noises some form of imminent danger. Even now, in my new house, I can almost hear the floors creaking, the ceiling closing in and drawing back again, in and out, as if it were breathing.

That night, when I saw the blood, I went back to my room. It was summer, and summer was always the noisiest time, because of the heat and the variation in temperature between day and night. I climbed back into bed with a wad of toilet paper in my underwear, because I knew this was only the beginning—though I had no idea yet of what was about to come. I had left the window open because of the heat, and I could see the light from the porch lamp; Grandma always left it on, for the dogs, who stayed out at night when the weather was warm enough, but also because she thought burglars would be more reluctant to approach a house if the lights were on. The house creaked under the weight of invisible footsteps. I stared at the ceiling and imagined that those footsteps belonged to my father, who was coming up from his room to sit on my bed, to lie down beside me and tell me there was nothing to be afraid of. I could feel the blood soaking the paper between my legs.

I woke up when daylight broke through the window. It must have been very early, because Grandma was still in bed. The sound of birdsong came from some faraway place, outside. The house was quiet. The crack in the wall across from my bed, running along an edge and halfway to the floor, had started to bleed.

MOTHER

GRANDMA USED TO TELL ME STORIES TO HELP ME FALL asleep, back when we still shared a room. We always went to bed first, together, soon after the evening programs started on television, and after my mother had made sure that I had brushed my teeth and that my pajamas were clean. She would look at them carefully, and sniff them, and pinch my neck and tickle my armpits, and the pajamas always smelled clean because unbeknownst to my mother, Grandma changed them once a week and laid them out to air every morning. When she was done with her inspection, my mother would give me a good-night kiss on the cheek, just like my father did. Grandma and I would get into our twin beds, separated by a bedside cabinet, and she would begin to talk. She spoke in a whisper, a low, constant murmur, the timbre of her voice becoming more similar to my mother's. Her stories were about the countryside, the house, the town, the world she knew. She told me stories about my mother when she was little, and of that time when she'd gone missing for three days and finally returned from the woods, her hair matted, her hands filthy with soil and blood, and never told anyone about where she'd been or how she'd managed to get lost, even though she knew that countryside better than anyone else did, and had always found her way home before.

"Were you scared?" I asked my grandmother.

"Yes," she said. "We all were. The whole town was out looking for her, down to the last man. We were convinced something bad had happened to her. We looked for her day and night, calling out her name. We were terrified, we were all terrified. Except for her. When she came back it was as if she'd come from a place she'd always known. I'll never forget her face. Her clothes all torn, scratches all over her legs, as if she'd been raised by wolves. She looked at us like we were strangers."

•

OVER THE YEARS I tried many times to ask my mother what had happened to her in the forest, where she'd slept, what she'd eaten. The house was surrounded by woods; sometimes my father took me for walks there. I had always been afraid of the woods, even before I'd heard the story of my mother's disappearance, but I would often ask my father to take me anyway. It's cold in there, even in high summer, and the air is damp and so laden with scents that it makes you dizzy. I pictured my mother there—all alone as the night crept up from the roots of the trees—and though I wanted to know how she'd survived it, and how she'd found her way back, I could never bring myself to ask. Occasionally we ran into someone on the street or received a visitor who brought it up; it was a well-known story in town—everyone had heard about it, and many had helped out with the search. My mother would bat the question away as if it were an irritating fly. She was really good at doing that: her interlocutor would quickly forget they'd even asked. She hadn't even told my father what had happened during those three days, and he had learned to respect her silence, just as he had learned to deal with every other aspect of her he could not control.

•

THEY HAD MET in high school. She was the girl from the blind house, the one who'd gone missing in the woods for three days: she was tall, with brown hair that reached down to her thighs, and big bright eyes that changed color depending on the weather—moss green on sunny days, hazel when the light was low, sometimes yellow like a cat's, staring right into yours when you spoke to her, then darting all over as if unable to be still for more than a moment. That was how my father described her. He was the veterinarian's son, and assisted his father when an animal was sick or giving birth. My grandfather had tried to teach him the job, but I don't think his son ever paid him much heed—except, I guess, when the job took them to Grandma's farm. He must have courted my mother for quite some time, even though she was not the type to let herself be courted. Or perhaps it had been the other way round. She had become pregnant soon after, when neither of them had expected it. They must have had other plans. She certainly had, with her dreams of going to university and leaving town—above all, of leaving that house. Her two elder sisters, my aunts, were already married and had children. One of them had three kids and lived in town; the other had moved to a residential neighborhood in the next town. Both of them had gone just far enough to get out of the place where they had been born, but not too far. They were older, much older than my mother; there were forty-two years between my grandmother and my mother. It was something my grandmother always reminded us about.

I doubt it was the life my mother would have wished for. My grandmother figured out straightaway that her daughter was pregnant, before my mother had decided what to do, before she'd even had a chance to consider her options. She had seen my mother come out of the shower one night—my mother often wandered around the house almost or completely naked, a habit my grandmother detested but could no longer forbid, though she had done so when my mother was little. She saw my mother's nipples and her belly and said: You're pregnant. That is how my mother tells it. From that moment on, my grandmother took charge. She quickly arranged their wedding, and my father moved into the house, into the room that had once been my grandparents'; neither he nor my mother had the means to find somewhere else to stay, not with a child on the way, and my grandmother certainly wasn't going to help them move to town, let alone farther away, as my mother would have wanted.

FATHER

THE DAY THE BLOOD CAME, I LEARNED HOW TO HIDE it. I blotted the crack in the wall with tissue paper and stuffed the paper in a plastic bag under the bed. This left an increasingly obvious copper-colored halo on the wall, so I took to locking the door every time I wasn't in the room. The rest of the blood, the kind that came from the wound between my legs, I dealt with the same way. I smuggled sanitary pads out of my mother's bathroom, one or two at a time so she wouldn't notice, and I tried to make them last. I couldn't just buy a new pack in town, in case someone might figure things out and tell my mother. I had to bide my time until it was her turn. Then she would send me to the shops to buy her some, and I would be able to buy more than one bag. I had also cut up an old cotton T-shirt to use in case there was too much blood. Grandma had told me that's what they used to do back when she was young.

But it was impossible to hide the blood on the wall for very long. My father was the one to spot it. He had already moved out by then, but he still visited often. He would spend whole afternoons with us and sometimes even stay for dinner, if my mother let him. He had begun to travel a lot for work; like almost half my peers' fathers, he worked in the ceramics industry, in one of the many tile factories situated on the stretch of highway ten kilometers north of town. When I was little he used to process orders at the factory, where he had his own office; in recent years they had started sending him on trips abroad, to negotiate with clients. To Eastern Europe, to Germany. He would go away for a few days, a week at most, and come back with gifts for me and for my mother, as well as some cheese or local sweets for my grandmother. My mother would make him tell her everything about his trips, asking him endless questions. I knew that she would have liked to go with him.

That day I had gone to take a shower in the big bathroom downstairs, accidentally leaving my bedroom door open. It happened on the fifth day, when the blood between my legs was about to cease, and the blood on the wall seemed to have faded with it. I think my father must have gone into my room to surprise me when I came back; he wasn't normally one to pry, not even when he noticed something unusual. Or maybe my mother had grown suspicious and sent him to check. I never found out. But when I finished in the bathroom and went back upstairs, I found him standing at the foot of the wall, his arms raised, wiping the blood with his fingers, prodding at the wall as if it were flesh.

I stood at the threshold, watching him, until he became aware of my presence.

"Did you see that?" he asked. "It looks like blood."

He was rubbing his red-stained fingertips together, thumb against index and middle finger, testing the thickness of the liquid.

"You hadn't noticed?"

I shook my head. He turned toward the wall again and stared up at the crack. "There must be a leak up there. Maybe a rusty pipe. It smells metallic."

He lifted his fingers to the crack again, following it with his index finger as far up as he could reach, before bringing it down to his nose. "Can you smell it? It really is like metal."

I stayed by the door and he walked toward me. "I should go and wash my hands," he said. "What did you do to your hair?" he added, peering at me.

I touched my head. "It's wet," I said. "I just took a shower."

"It looks longer. It suits you. You look different. Older."

There was a hint of a stain on his nose, a red shadow on his nostrils. He rubbed at it when I pointed it out. My mother always said my nose was exactly like my father's: round but with the tip bending downward just a tiny bit, giving us a vaguely comical appearance, like eaglets. And our expression: wide-eyed, she said, as if we were forever expecting to be praised or reproved. Large, slanted eyes, black like dogs' eyes, so dark you had to be out in the light and get really close if you wanted to see our pupils. Mom used to say that my father had never had to ask her for anything. All she had to do was look at him, sitting by a window and staring out or walking with his hands in the pockets of the oversized jean jacket he wore when he was younger, his gaze turned to the floor or up at the sky—she liked how he was always looking either too high up or too low down, his lips dark and turned downward, like a girl's, his expression distracted and melancholy, as if he'd absorbed years' worth of fog and hoarfrost. My mother used to say that's how he got all the girls: he never had to ask, never even had to try. Not all the girls, mind you: only those who paid attention. They came and then they drifted away again without him ever knowing the reason.

He smiled now as he rubbed his nose and left the room. "See you tomorrow?" he said.

"Are you leaving already?"

He nodded. "I'll tell Enzo to come and have a look. At the leak, I mean."

"No," I piped up. "I'll take care of it. I'm going to town with Grandma today. You know what she's like. He'll come straightaway if she asks."

"All right then," he said. He started to go, but then he paused. "I almost forgot: I got you something."

He turned around and smiled, squinting like he was trying to wink at me but couldn't quite manage it.

"What is it?" I said.

"Come with me."

I followed him downstairs. "Where is it?" I asked.

"In the car. Come."

Next to the car, in the farmyard we used as a parking lot, my mother was playing with a puppy. It was jumping up and down, biting at her hands.

"Is that what you got me?" I squealed. "Is he really mine?"

My mother picked it up and handed it to me.

"It's yours," she said. "Ours."

"It's a she," my father said. "Go on, pick her up."

I crouched down to do so. She looked like a German shepherd puppy, but smaller and less graceful. Her paws were too large for her body. She licked my face and nibbled my hair. She looked like a kangaroo.

"She's beautiful," I said. "Thank you." She nipped at my nose and acted like she was happy to meet me. She seemed to like me.

"She's three months old," said my father. "You must take care of her."

"I will," I said.

"You'd better," said my mother. "Or else your father will take her back. Isn't that right?"

We brought her into the house and gave her something to eat. My grandma appeared and watched us in silence, holding back her older dog, Luna, who was excitedly sniffing the air. "So is it a female?" Grandma asked, holding Luna by her collar.

"Yes," my father replied. "You can let her go."

Grandma narrowed her eyes and peered at the puppy's belly to see for herself, as if she didn't trust him, then let go of the collar. Luna ran toward the puppy but stopped a yard short. She studied her from that distance before moving closer. We were all watching to see how she would react. Luna seemed not to have any objections. She sniffed the puppy all over, and the puppy did the same to her. Luna observed the puppy eating for a while, then walked off.

"What are you going to call her?" my father asked.

"I don't know," I answered. "I need to think about it properly."

We watched her eat from Luna's bowl. She seemed to have a healthy appetite.

"This is your dog now," Grandma said. "It's your job to look after it. You're old enough. If you don't, your father will take it back."

•

I WASN'T ALLOWED to take her to bed with me. "Animals are animals," said Grandma. "They must stay outside at night, and we can't make an exception for her."

"But she's so small!" I protested.

"Luna will keep her company. She's had puppies before— she will remember what to do."

In bed, I kept thinking about it; I kept thinking about a

name for her but couldn't make my mind up. As I lay there, my eyes open in the dark, I remembered the crack in the wall.

That night, I prayed for my father to forget about it. I kneeled by the bed, joining my hands together on the mattress. It had been a long time since I'd prayed, but I still remembered how it was done. I prayed that my father would never mention it to my grandmother or to my mother. I prayed that he would never ask me about the wall. I prayed for the blood to stop coming, and for no one to ever speak of it.

In a way, my prayers were answered.

MOTHER'S MOTHER

THE BLOOD STOPPED COMING, FROM THE WALL first, then from my body. It left a trace on the wall that changed color every day, like a bruise: copper, then crimson, then a purplish hue, then blue, green. That was difficult to hide. My grandmother noticed around ten days later, when it had begun to look like nothing more than a patch of mold, only slightly redder. She saw it while cleaning one morning when I was outside with Mom. I'd stopped locking the door by then in case they should grow suspicious, and anyway I thought the danger had passed. When we returned, we found Grandma sitting on my bed, staring at the crack.

"Mom, what's wrong?" my mother said. I held my breath, waiting on the landing, the door to my room open, the crack in the wall nothing more than a harmless shadow from where I stood.

"Up there," my grandmother rasped, pointing. "Look."

My mother moved closer. "It's mold. What was the fix for that? Bleach or ammonia? I can never remember."

Grandma remained still, her gaze still upturned.

"Mom?" my mother called out. "Have you fallen asleep?"

Grandma shook her head. "It's not mold," she said. "It looks like plague. A plague in the house."

My mother laughed. "What on earth are you talking about?"

Grandma took her eyes away from the wall and turned them on my mother, as if she were trying to see her more clearly.

My mother averted her gaze. "It's only mold, Mom," she said. "I'll wipe it off with bleach. Are you feeling well?"

Grandma shook her head. "No. You're right. I think I need to rest," she said. She stood up, refusing my mother's outstretched hand. She walked down the stairs and into her room, shut the door behind herself, and did not come out until evening.

"I'm worried," my mother said around dinnertime. "I've never seen her like that. I called her a quarter of an hour ago and she still hasn't come down."

I had walked past my grandma's room that afternoon. I had walked past it five times at half-hour intervals, and on three occasions I had heard her praying. I knew what she did when she prayed: she picked up the garnet rosary she kept hanging from the mirror on her dressing table, kneeled by the bed with her elbows planted on the edge and her hands clasped together, and counted out prayers, the rosary beads clattering as they slowly sank onto the bed. When I was little she would make me kneel beside her and we would pray together. The rosary, though, I wasn't allowed to touch: that was hers to hold, her gnarled hands marking out a quick, steady rhythm on the crimson beads. We used to pray together before bedtime, when we still slept in the same room, and even after that, up until my First Communion, I would pray with Grandma every night before going up to my room in the attic. I was around ten or eleven when the ritual started to bore me, and soon enough, so did Sunday school. I asked my mother to stop sending me, and it was as if the moment she'd been waiting for had finally arrived: she hadn't set foot in church since her wedding day, never prayed, and would periodically announce that she didn't believe in God, just to spite Grandma. Until then she hadn't dared contradict my grandmother on anything concerning my education. But from that day on, she finally had the excuse she needed, for it had been my idea after all, not hers. This was the year when all my classmates were preparing for their confirmation. Grandma didn't take it well; I could hear them arguing all the way up in the attic room after my father had gone to bed, with Grandma blaming my mother, blaming it on her inadequacy, her hostility. First she yelled; then she begged. You must give her a chance to be saved, she would say. My mother would reply that there was nothing to be saved from. She is different from you, Grandma would say, and thank God for that. You know she is different, and you cannot abide it, so now you are trying to drag her toward your path, just as you always do. You try to make people more like you because it is the only way you know how to be less alone.

Then she would go back upstairs to her room, and if I went down and stood quietly outside her door, I would hear her pray. My mother would stay downstairs. She would stay there for a long time. She would cry. Sometimes I thought I could hear her struggling to breathe.

My grandma had her way in the end. I went back to Sunday school. I went back to believing that if I didn't, my soul would turn black; I would die and end up in hell, where I would spend eternity in darkness and silence, alone. I began preparing for my confirmation again, and every night before going to sleep I pretended to pray, alternating every line of prayer with all the swear words and blasphemous curses I knew, and asking in the same breath for the Virgin Mary's forgiveness.

•

MY MOTHER WIPED the stain with bleach, as she'd told Grandma she would. But once wasn't enough; the outline soon became visible again. So she took to scrubbing it twice a day, for five days. She was meticulous about it, sponging at the wall with a wet washcloth, all the way into the corners, as if everything depended on the care she put into the task. She did it herself, without any help from Enzo, though of course he'd offered. Enzo lived a few houses up the road, even farther from town than we did, and regularly dropped by. He helped out with any chores that might need doing in the house or out in the fields. There were certain things my father wasn't very good at—trimming the hedges, repairing fences, shearing the sheep. His hands were small and soft, unlike those of his own father, the veterinarian. My father saw this as a blessing; his father saw it as a disgrace. Enzo, though, could do pretty much everything. Every time he came by, he brought a bottle of wine or a jar of the honey he made himself. In exchange he would take eggs, milk, or some cheese. He would visit once or twice a week, but sometimes more and without any warning. This angered my grandmother. He was a widower, and my mother sometimes teased my grandmother that if it were up to him, he would come every day. Grandma would always turn very formal around him and treat him coldly—barely speaking, her tone dry, her movements measured—as if his very presence there irritated her.

But he was indispensable, and we knew it. Grandma knew it, and my mother knew it, no matter how reluctant they both were to admit it. There are certain things a woman can't sort out by herself: that's what people would tell my grandma when she went to the hardware store in town to buy a can of paint or replacement blades for the mower; it was what they'd say to my mother when she stopped to talk to other parents outside school or in town and they asked her how Grandma managed to keep the farm running after my grandfather's death and with no one to help her, except for the two young men she occasionally hired to clean the stables and the cages or to pick fruit. Both of them would shrug their shoulders and smile, as if to say, And yet here we are. My mother was different: she had fewer qualms about asking for help and accepting her helplessness whenever it manifested itself, and she had learned to turn her condition to her advantage. But they were loath to accept the help Enzo offered, both for the same reason: they saw it as a sign of surrender. I think deep down my mother expected more of my grandmother than she let on, as if in her mind, no matter how many mistakes she herself committed, no matter how many weaknesses she admitted to, Grandma would always be there to hold everything together.

My mother bleached the wall two times a day and the room took on a cold, white smell, like hospitals or snow. I took a deep breath every time I walked in, and stood on my toes beneath the crack to breathe it in some more. Sometimes the smell was so strong that I felt faint, and if I paid close enough attention I could feel it go through my nose and throat straight into my lungs, past my heart. I did this as often as I could, for as long as the smell stayed, because I was sure that it would make me clean.

•

"SO. HAVE YOU decided what to call her?" my mother asked.

"Neve," I said. "I will call her Neve, like snow."

"But she looks nothing like snow. She's black and brown."

"I like it."

"Has she been spayed?" my grandmother asked.

"I don't know," my mother replied. "I didn't ask."

"I think she might be too young still," Grandma said. "Let

me see." She picked the dog up and examined her belly. "Yes, just as I thought."

"Will we need to get her spayed?" I asked. "Why?"

"Because there will be hell to pay if we don't," my mother replied. "She'll churn out babies one after another, like a rabbit. We'd have to open a puppy farm."

"It would be best to let her have at least one litter first," said Grandma.

"Why is that?"

"For her own good. It's healthier that way."

TWO

IT WAS AFTER THE STAIN FADED AND THE SMELL OF bleach receded from my room that they began to turn up. Not all at once, but little by little. At first it was funny. I would pick them up between two fingers, grasping them gently, so as not to hurt them, just above their hind legs. Their skin was fleshy, cold but not unpleasantly so. I would find them on the porch at night or hiding in the lawn, scattered here and there among the grass. I would nudge them out of the way with my foot or pick them up and drop them close to the lake, where I was convinced they came from. Then they began to multiply. I could hear them croaking at night, beneath my bedroom window. We would find the frogs piled up on the porch in the morning, large greenish blurs shifting with every breath, trembling like leaves, vibrating with the flow of their own cold blood. Grandma said she'd never in her life seen so many. We had to keep the windows and doors shut for fear they might come inside the house.

My mother no longer left her room. She had stepped on one by mistake; it had become impossible to avoid them. The frog had wilted like a punctured balloon, sticking to the stone floor of the porch, its innards splayed around. The smell had attracted Neve, who had dashed over and started nuzzling the carcass. My mother had screamed, and from that moment on, she had refused to come out. She spent the whole day in her bedroom now, the door closed, the shutters sealed.

Grandma tried to open the shutters to let some light in. "They can't reach all the way up here anyway," she said.

But my mother stopped her with a shake of her head. "I have a headache," she said. "It's that neck pain again."

We brought her breakfast and lunch. She came out only in the evenings, when all the shutters in the house were closed, and we had dinner together. She was becoming ever more pale. My father's visits had become less frequent: they had gone down to twice a week, then only once a week, on Sundays. When the number of frogs increased, he became alarmed.

"I've never seen so many," he said, looking around wide-eyed, his arms crossed over his chest as if he was worried that he might be attacked.

"It's the heat," Grandma said. "The humidity. It's the muggiest summer I can remember."

"I don't think so," said my father, shaking his head. "There isn't a single frog over at my place, or anywhere else. This croaking . . . you should call pest control."

Grandma huffed. "What good would they be? They wouldn't do anything we're not already doing. We like to take care of things ourselves here," she said.

My father averted his eyes, then turned to look at me, at the opposite end of the porch. I returned his gaze, wishing he'd come over to hug me. But instead he turned back around, his eyes roaming again. "I don't know how you can stand the noise," he said.

"You get used to it eventually," said Grandma. "You stop hearing it after a while. Grin and bear it. If you even know what that means."

She smoothed her apron and started making her way back inside. On the threshold, she turned around and caught my eye. "Don't worry, Valentina. It won't last long. They'll be gone soon."

She was right, in a sense. My father left that day, giving me a kiss on the forehead, and I had a feeling that it would be the last time.

"There's something I need to tell you, Vale," he said, his hand still resting on the back of my head. I could feel his fingers through my hair. They felt heavy. "I'm going away next week. I'll be gone for a while, for work."

"Where are you going?" I asked.

"To Russia. They're sending me to Moscow to deal with some clients there."

"That's really far," I said, with the slightest shake of my head, hoping he'd remove his hand. He did. "How long will you stay for?"

"A while. Maybe a few months."

"Take me with you," I said.

"I can't. You know your mother needs you."

"Take me with you now. Just for tonight."

He smiled and kissed me again, patting Neve's head. "Next time," he said. He was wearing a shirt my mother and I had gotten him for his birthday the year before. I felt like crying, and clenched my fists until I could feel my nails digging into my palms. The tears stayed put.

There were so many frogs now that it had become difficult to walk. My mother still wouldn't leave her bedroom, and my grandma would shove the frogs off with her feet or kick them away, cursing as she walked back and forth between the vegetable garden and the orchard. Though she wouldn't admit it, I knew she was as disgusted as my mother was. Even the dogs, who had been attracted by the frogs at first, were staying away now. They watched the creatures from a distance, no longer going up to sniff them, and ventured outside only when they had to relieve themselves.

As for me, I would go out onto the meadow barefoot and wait for the frogs to come hopping over my feet. I would pick them up and study them up close, inspecting their skin, that color somewhere between green and brown, with darker patches here and there, and the thin, shiny, yellowish line running down the middle of their backs. They had four thin toes on each foot, and at the end of each toe was a small sphere, like E.T.'s fingers. Their skin was creased and uneven, like Grandma's. I would lift them up in the air until their tiny, bulging eyes were level with mine. I would stare at them and make sure they were staring back at me. At first their eyelids would flutter, so I would tell them not to worry, that nothing bad would happen. I would stroke their bellies gently so that they would learn to trust me. Then I would begin to tighten my grip. They would start to pee. Their eyelids would flutter again, slowly at first, then faster, then stop altogether, as if they had suddenly become as heavy as rocks, impossible to lift. I had discovered a particular spot on their chest, corresponding roughly to where their heart or lungs must be, that if I squeezed in just the right way, with some force but not enough to squash them, the frogs would stop breathing without even realizing it. Their skin would sag then and turn even softer and more elastic. Sometimes, after their eyes had already closed, I would hold them with two fingers—my thumb on their abdomen and my index finger on their back—and I would squeeze hard, to see how far I could go until I crushed them entirely. Then I would walk toward the lake, though not quite to the shore, and throw them as far as I could, challenging myself to hit the water. Or else I would dig a hole and dump them inside. I would gather a few of them together, cover them with earth, and mark the spot with a little cross made of twigs and twine. Pretty soon much of the field was covered in crosses, so small you could hardly see them, concealed among the tall grass.

I would lie down in the meadow, positioning myself against the breeze, letting my skirt lift up, the air caressing my skin in a steady rhythm. Sometimes I would pull my underwear down, just a tiny bit, and start to touch myself, surrounded by frogs oblivious to what was happening. They would leap to and fro, croaking, moving closer and closer. At first they would pause at what seemed a safe distance, but soon they would come nearer, until they were hopping over my stomach, my feet, my shoulders. I would stay where I was, lying down, touching myself until I had to close my eyes because the light was too bright. Then I would get up and start playing my game again. The frogs that had walked over my body, I spared.

•

THE FROGS LASTED for ten days. Then they stopped coming—just as gradually as when they had first appeared. I thought my game must have worked. The croaking lessened. They began to die, just a few of them first, until suddenly they were all dying, one after the other, as if they'd been struck by some epidemic disease. We found them everywhere: on trees, inside vases, in the tool shed, in the cracks between the flagstones. There seemed to be even more of them than we'd thought. Some had managed to sneak into the house, and for days we kept finding their remains behind doors, under wardrobes, in the bathroom. They began to rot, and the heat, which had grown fiercer in the meantime, hastened their decomposition, the stench spreading all over the house and contaminating the air. Grandma spent all her time cleaning: she washed the floors twice a day, the water so thick with detergent that every time she plunged the washcloth inside, bubbles would form and float in the air until they burst. She aired the rooms, sprayed perfumes, and lit incense sticks. "It's like an exorcism," my mother snickered—having meanwhile decided that her headache had passed and it was time to get out of bed, change the sheets in every room, and dust off all the furniture, destroying as many frogs as possible in the process.

Her bedroom was the only place the frogs had never reached. I thought it must be because she had kept the door and windows shut and barricaded herself in there. She'd done a good job of it, better than Grandma, whose room had been breached, the frogs hiding under the bed, on her dressing table, among her prayer cards and rosaries. There they lay in wait, neither eating nor drinking, until someone, or until death, came to claim them.

•

EVEN THOUGH THE number of frogs was diminishing, their croaking—which came from the garden and entered through my window—seemed louder than before. Sometimes it would wake me up in the middle of the night. The muggy air was fouled by the putrid smell of their corpses rotting in some hidden corner we hadn't been able to root them out of, the odor mixing with the incense to form a dense, pungent trail that I can still smell today when mowed grass begins to mold on a humid day. I lay awake with my eyes fixed on the ceiling, listening to that wet, full, slippery sound, which seemed to originate from some dark and hidden place. I would lie on my back with my legs curled against my chest, for fear that a frog might come in and hop onto me. Sometimes when I closed my eyes I could see my mother. She was standing by my bed; I could feel her presence over me. She was cradling a frog larger, much larger, than all the rest. I could hear its foaming, gurgling croak, like some sputtering, simmering liquid. My mother leaned over me and said: Look at me, Valentina. You'd better look at me. You brought them here. You know how to make them go away.

I kept my eyes shut. After a while, she went away, and I could go back to sleep.

THREE

IN THE SUMMER MY MOTHER ALWAYS WOKE UP either too late or too early. She wore long, wispy dresses, the thin linen or cotton fabric—white, blue, light green, pale pink—floating behind her as she came down the stairs or stepped through the French doors. When she woke up early— before Grandma, maybe even before dawn—she would go out into the garden. I would see her through the window some- times, when it was still dark outside, and it would take me a while to fall asleep again. She would go out barefoot and get to work in the vegetable garden, where Grandma would soon join her. She had never been afraid of the dark, of the garden, of the animals that might sneak in at night through some hole in the fence—foxes, beech martens, stray dogs. Inside the house, and on our land, she moved with the conviction that nothing bad could ever happen to her. And nothing ever had. I think the animals must have been able to sense it just as they can sense fear; they could sense the calmness, the decisiveness, the ease with which she moved through what was her home, had always been her home—all of which lent her an air of authority. It was how I saw her every time I tried to picture her in the woods, those three days she'd spent there when she was little.

On days when she woke up late, she would come down while I was having breakfast, or sitting outside in the garden, or doing my summer homework at the dining table on the porch. I would hear her coming down the stairs, and there she would be, her billowing dress making her seem like some fairy-tale creature capable of flight. She would greet me by stroking my hair, or sometimes, when I was younger and she was in the mood, with a volley of kisses. Sometimes she would kiss me on the lips, a fleeting touch that would give me shivers all over and make me wish she would do it again. That particular mark of affection was forbidden to my father. It's not appropriate, my mother would say. But she could easily take exception to much less than that—if I spent too much time with him, or if she found us cuddled up on the sofa, reading a book. "Come here, Valentina," she would say, inventing some urgent task I needed to attend to. She would use my full name, instead of the shortened form she usually called me by. She did that whenever she wanted to scold me for something, whenever I did anything I wasn't supposed to do, or when she felt she needed to assert her authority.

Sometimes she would put me in front of the mirror, the one above the bathroom sink or the one over the dressing table in her bedroom. She'd sit me on the bed and perch beside me. Look, she would say. Look at your forehead and your mouth. This little dimple on your chin. You look just like me. If it wasn't for your nose, you'd look just like me. Your grandmother always says that girls take after their fathers. But that's bullshit, and you're proof of that. You're right, I said bullshit. Let it be our little secret. She would sit there staring at my reflection in the mirror, delighting in how much I looked like her. As if that was all she'd ever wanted, as if it was what she'd secretly prayed for every day, something she'd done everything in her power to bring about. As if during all that time I'd spent inside her womb, she had thought of nothing else.

It was during a moment like this that I first noticed the mosquito bites on her arms, and the red scratch marks all around them.

"It's terrible, isn't it?" she said when she saw that I'd noticed. "They must have come in while I was sleeping last night. I'm so itchy," she said, scratching vigorously at her skin. "They got to your grandma, too." She looked at me. "Nothing on you?"

She checked my arms, my legs, then pulled my dress up to look at my stomach and back as I tried to wriggle away.

"Keep still," she said. "Don't tell me you're too shy now to let your own mother look at you?"

I stopped trying to get away and held my body rigid. Maybe the easiest thing to do was to let her have her way, so it would be over sooner and she wouldn't ask too many questions.

"Look at you," she said. "You're a young lady now. Let me see here."

She lifted my arms up to check my armpits. I knew I had no hair at all there yet, except for a couple I checked every morning, my face inches from the mirror. She tickled me, then pushed my arms back down. She was smiling. I looked at her in the mirror and she seemed different. Not uglier, just different. I wondered if the mirror actually changed people every time it showed their reflection. I wondered if my appearance, too, was different from the way I thought I looked.

"It's almost time," my mother said, suddenly serious again. "You know it's almost time, don't you?"

"Almost time for what?" I asked, though I already knew what she meant.

"Don't let your grandmother scare you. When I was your age I'd already had them for two years, maybe even longer than that. She wouldn't even let me wash my hair."

"So is it all right to do that?"

"She would look at me like I was a blight. I was nine and a half, I was too young. If it had been up to her, she would have locked me up somewhere, like a dog in heat," she said, shaking her head before looking at me again. "It's always too soon when it starts," she said, stroking my knee. She got up, and the mattress rose with her. "And once it's there, you can't change it back. It's the same with time. It's the same with anything that happens. If only we could," she said, and walked out of the room.

•

WITHIN A WEEK, the number of mosquitoes had begun to multiply. They had always troubled us more in the summer when the weather got hot, and Grandma would line the porch with mosquito coils and lemon-colored candles, which she lit up as soon as it got dark outside. But when I saw the bites on my mother's skin I realized that the mosquitoes were bigger and more numerous than usual that year. They bothered us during the day, too, and bit us constantly, especially when we were out in the vegetable garden or in the fields. We had no choice but to cover ourselves in mosquito repellent. I remember those days by the smell of citronella, its sweet, pungent scent filling up my nostrils and dulling all the other senses.

My father left. He came to see us one Sunday, the day before he was due to set off. It was one of the saddest days of my life, at least up to that point. I stayed glued to him all day, sitting on his lap, hugging him. I was angry, but I couldn't bring myself to avoid him—I wanted to stock up on him in preparation for when he wouldn't be around. He scolded me for scratching at a mosquito bite on my ankle, one of many. "It'll get infected," he said. "Besides, I've told you, the more you scratch them, the more they'll itch."

"I know," I said. "But I can't stop doing it."

He wet his finger with his tongue, then gently rubbed at

the bite, massaging delicately. "There," he said. "Just try to resist for a minute, and you'll see it won't itch anymore. You have my word."

•

IT WAS SOMEWHERE around that time—July, August 1996—that I met Marco. Ilaria, my best friend, had just come back from her holidays, and we were lying on the lawn in the courtyard one afternoon. I had introduced her to Neve, pleased to have something new to talk to her about. Neve had licked her hands, as she did with everyone, then started fussing until we played with her. We had scratched her belly and thrown an old stuffed toy of mine—a dog—which she had now claimed for herself. Neve had run to fetch it but hadn't brought it back; she was holding it between her paws, chewing at it furiously with those new teeth of hers, so small and sharp.

"Look what you've done," I said. "You've ripped it to shreds."

"You're murdering your own child!" said Ilaria.

I laughed. "It's true, she's eating her own kind."

"You cannibal!"

"Shame on you," I said. "You have no respect for your offspring."

Afterward we let ourselves fall back onto the grass, and Ilaria—her skin the color of tea biscuits, her brown hair sun-bleached at the tips—had begun to tell me about the weeks she had spent at her grandparents' house in Sardinia. I pretended to listen, but actually I'd stopped following the words she was saying a while ago, and had become fixated on her face, the way she moved her lips and hands, and how much all of it seemed to have changed since the last time we had seen each other. Ilaria had had this particular way of gesticulating, as if she had to sketch everything she was talking about or sculpt it out of clay, because she had always had a little trouble with words, and they never seemed to be enough. She had also always had a terrible habit of bringing her hands to her mouth and biting her cuticles every time she stopped talking, so that her fingers would look awful, her half-eaten nails white and flat like pebbles. But now that skin was smooth and clear, her nails painted light blue. She moved her hands slowly, floating them through the air as if she were following some current, and though she was still talking nonstop, there was a calmness about her, as if she didn't really care about choosing the right word because she already knew what it was that she had to say.

"I know, right?" she said when she noticed what I was looking at. "My mother made me promise I'd stop. She said she'll put a TV in my room if I stop biting my cuticles. I haven't touched them in two weeks."

"Well done," I said, trying to act like I cared. I could hear my mother's and my grandmother's voices from the porch. They were assembling a mosquito trap Enzo had bought in the city. It was a cage with a tube of fluorescent light inside; it worked by attracting insects and then electrocuting them. I turned to look at Ilaria again. "How did you do it?"

"I found this in a shop. It smells like cat piss. There's no way I can bite them now. Look."

She brought her fingers up to my nose, and I breathed in. I had smelled that scent somewhere before, though I couldn't remember where. It was a bitter, wet smell, like old lemons, but with a trace of sweetness to it.

"It's awful, isn't it?" she said, laughing. "Though now I almost like it. I get the urge to sniff it sometimes."

She folded her fingers and lifted them to her nose. "See? This is what I do when I want to smell it in secret."

She stayed that way for a moment, curled up on herself, then quickly drew her hand away. "I haven't told anyone else. I haven't even told Sara."

"Who's Sara?" I asked. I nudged Neve with my leg; she had tired of tormenting the stuffed toy and had turned her attention to my foot.

"The girl I met on the beach. She's a year older than we are. I had seen her around before, but this summer we became friends. She's the one who told me about the nail polish," she said, glancing at me.

"Does she live there?" I asked.

"No, she's from Milan. Near Milan, she said. She goes on holiday to the same place every year. Her parents have a house there. The boys I was telling you about earlier are her friends. She's known them ever since she was little, so she introduced them to me."

"Did you go to the beach with them?"

"Yes, I told you. And we also met up in the evenings. Oh, and we went into town, too."

"Did they have a car?"

"No, but they have mopeds. Though my parents didn't

want me to get on. And Sara doesn't have a moped. So Mom and Dad drove me there and Sara came with us."

I nodded, twisting a blade of grass around my finger, then ripping it off.

"Ouch," she said.

"What?"

"I just got bit by a mosquito."

"Serves you right," I said. "I told you they're everywhere. You should have used the spray."

"Thanks, Mom," she said, narrowing her eyes at me.

"Oh, I'm sorry. I bet no one ever told you what to do when you were down in Sardinia."

I hunched my shoulders and turned away from her. We were quiet for a time, until it got to be too much. I looked at her again. I could tell when she was angry from the way she frowned. We had that in common, according to my father.

I blew a raspberry at her to make her look. Then I smiled at her.

Ilaria hugged me. She could never sulk at me for long. It had been that way since we were little. "Idiot," she said. "I missed you."

I pinched her arm. "I'm a mosquito," I said. She laughed.

I would have liked to tell her about what had happened while she was away, about the blood, and about my father. I would have liked to ask her if I seemed different. I tried to figure out where to start, but I couldn't think of anything, and felt an ache rising in my stomach. So I decided I wouldn't tell her, not yet anyway, not unless she asked. It's not like they say it is, I thought; sometimes, things do disappear if you pretend they never happened. It was just a matter of staying strong, of keeping the secret, and everything would go away.

We stayed on the lawn for a while, talking about music and the films we'd seen; we talked as if the time we'd spent apart had never existed, and I forgot about everything that had happened. We got up to go to the kitchen, where my grandmother fed us iced tea and ice cream sandwiches. The mosquito cage buzzed intermittently. "Every time you hear that noise, it's a mosquito dying. One less thing to worry about," said Grandma. "You'll see how many there will be when it gets dark tonight. They're attracted to light, like all animals."

Ilaria and I finished our iced tea and ice cream and went back out, down the hill and onto the road that led to town. Ilaria and her parents lived in town, in a row of terraced houses that had been built when we were little. I still remember the construction site: I would walk past it with Grandma on our way to the shops, when I was around five or six, or with my father on our way back from the market on Saturday mornings after we'd gone to visit my mother at our family stall. I remember watching the houses coming into existence bit by bit, rising from their foundations, the beams growing and the walls closing until you could no longer see what was inside unless you peered through the windows. But I also remember that it seemed to go on for such a long time, as it if might never end. "When will they finish?" I asked my father, who smiled and replied, "It's not like making a farm out of Legos. These buildings have to be strong enough to withstand the wind, the rain, and the passage of time. It's a difficult task."

Back then Ilaria had still lived in the city, where she was

born. She moved to our town with her parents when the construction work was completed. We were in second grade when she arrived. I remember that on the first day of school she came into the classroom and we all stared at her as she sat down at a desk in the back row. None of us had ever seen her before, which was a new experience in a town like ours: we'd all gone to the same preschool, and we'd gotten to know the older kids from seeing them in the school halls, or else their parents were friends with ours. We thought she must have gotten the wrong classroom. She avoided our stares but did not look down. When the teacher arrived, she told her to introduce herself. Ilaria just said her name and fell silent again, didn't even stand up, and the teacher had to explain where she was from, why she'd switched schools, and how she would be our classmate from now on.

I watched her in the days that followed, when she hadn't spoken to anyone yet. Sometimes I thought she looked sad, and other times it seemed as if she didn't mind being on her own. She would draw wherever she felt like it: on her notebooks, on the plastic jackets that covered all our textbooks, on the backs of books, even on the desk, during class. One day I went up to her and told her I really liked her drawings. I was standing; she was sitting at her desk. I watched her as I waited for her to say something, and I felt grown-up; I experienced for the first time the feeling of having made the right move. I knew how she was feeling: she had been waiting for days for someone to talk to her—really talk to her, that is. When she looked up and into my eyes, saying nothing, her pencil hovering over a piece of paper, I realized there was something inside her that I knew, that I knew very well, and it was a comforting thought. I think she must have felt something similar too, though we never spoke about it. I felt guilty for not having seen it before; in that moment and in the days that followed, as my friendship with Ilaria grew until we became inseparable, I felt guilty for having only approached her because no one else had done it yet; I felt guilty for how proud of myself I had been when I had decided I would finally go over and acknowledge her. That, I thought, is what you get for doing what you're told to do. That's what it feels like when you do what everyone wishes you would do, what everyone expects you to do. Being good makes you arrogant, and it makes you weak, so I decided I would never fall into the trap again.

Ilaria was the only girl I knew who hadn't been baptized. Neither had her brother. Their parents had been married in the town hall, not in church. They believed in homeopathy, tried to eat healthy, and walked around the house barefoot. They'd left the city because the air quality was better here; they kept a little vegetable garden and bought the rest of their food from us, because they trusted my grandmother and knew she didn't use any artificial pesticides. They didn't eat meat, though they did feed it to their children occasionally, and every time they visited us, they would look at our animals with eyes full of compassion. They tried to ingratiate themselves with my grandma by buying her produce, and I think they looked up to her with something like fearful reverence, though she never enjoyed their visits and did not approve of my friendship with Ilaria. But her Catholicism prevented her from being too interfering, so she limited herself to treating them coldly, even more so than she treated everyone else. She was polite, she spoke no more words than those strictly required, and she gave away no smiles: that way she didn't have to hide from anyone, and no one could hold anything against her.

•

WE REACHED THE main road that led to town. Ilaria would cycle the whole length of it when her mother was at work and couldn't drop her off. The tar was still fresh, and in parts a brilliant black that looked wet. By contrast, the road I lived on was narrow and uneven, the asphalt years old and worn along the edges, full of potholes and covered in dust. There were only three other houses on our road, apart from ours—and Enzo's, which marked the end of the road. The families that lived there had children who were older than me; I had played with them for years, when I was younger, until the age difference no longer allowed it.

We knew Marco by sight, just like we knew everyone else. He was a year older than we were, in the final year of middle school. You noticed him because he was loud during recess, he played pranks on the girls, and if you went to the bathroom during class it wasn't unusual to bump into him in the hallway, where he'd been banished as punishment. He was cycling toward us that day, perhaps on his way back from town. He was pedaling fast, right in the middle of the road. He saw us from a distance before we saw him. Ilaria was wheeling her bike along and I was walking next to her. Marco cycled past us, then came to a sudden stop, his brakes screeching.

"What's up with the rocket?" he said. He tilted his chin toward Ilaria's bike, which was old and faded compared to his. "Is it a puncture?"

"No," she replied with a shrug. "My rocket is just fine."

"Then why aren't you riding it?"

"Because there's two of us and just one bike," she said. "Are you blind?"

"Big deal," he said, lifting his front wheel. "I'll tell you a secret: your friend can sit on the back. Ever tried that, princess?"

"What about you, princess?" said Ilaria in a singsong voice, as if she were talking to a two-year-old. "Ever tried minding your own fucking business?"

Marco burst out laughing. I admired Ilaria for how she'd managed to reply to him, and how quickly. I hadn't said a word yet. I was just "her friend."

"Wow, you're crabby," Marco teased. "I guess it must be that time of the month. Maybe that's why you won't get on the bike. You're worried you'll stain your cute little shorts red."

I was petrified. I glanced at Ilaria, feeling a wave of heat rising inside me. Her mouth dropped open for a moment. "That's disgusting!" she screamed, glaring at him. "All right then. You asked for it."

"Oooh," he said. "Now I'm scared!"

"Let's see who makes it to town first."

Marco laughed again, louder this time. "You're not serious. Do you really think you can beat me, with those stick legs you've got?"

"I'll show you."

"All right then, princess. Starting positions." He moved toward us with the bike between his legs and his feet on the ground. "What about your friend? Are we leaving her here?"

"I live back there," I said.

"I know where you live," he said, looking at me. "In the blind house."

There was a silence, or so it seemed to me, until Ilaria intervened: "She'll come with me. She can sit on the back. Two against one."

He laughed. "No way! You don't stand a chance—I'll be in town before you've even started."

"Women are stronger," said Ilaria.

"You'll have a pretty terrible time of it, you know that, right?"

"You wish," said Ilaria, though she was regretting it already. But I'd had an idea: "Why don't *you* take me, then, if you're so good," I said.

Marco snorted. "Oh sure, how convenient. You're penalizing me."

"Don't tell me you're having second thoughts," said Ilaria. "If you think you're better than me, you should be able to win either way, penalty or no penalty. You're a boy, and you're older."

"All right, all right. Hop on, princess number two."

There was no back seat on his bike, so I would have to climb up onto the handlebar. I'd already tried that before on my father's bike, and I remembered how uncomfortable it was. I tried again now, and it wasn't comfortable with Marco's, either. "I'll crack my head open if you brake," I protested.

In the end we decided to switch: Marco and I would take Ilaria's bike, and Ilaria would take his.

"For the record, that counts as a double penalty. I get the dead weight and the old wreck. You're getting a Ferrari," he told Ilaria. "You'd better take good care of it."

"I'm not dead weight," I said. I wanted to punch him in the back. He was wearing a thin T-shirt, and every time he leaned forward, I could see the shape of his spine.

"And that is not an old wreck," said Ilaria.

"Sure it isn't," he said, swatting at his own arm. "Will you hurry up and get on? The mosquitoes are eating me alive. What the hell is this place?"

"They're killing me, too," Ilaria moaned. "Look," she said, showing us her arm covered with bites. They were enormous, red and swollen from scratching.

"You must have really sweet blood," said Marco, batting his eyelashes.

"I'm ready," I said. I could smell the yellow scent of the bug spray wafting from my arms. Maybe it would protect him, too. Maybe I could protect him.

Marco and Ilaria stood side by side, taking care to stay on the same imaginary starting line. I started them off, and he began to pedal. He was fast, and I could see his back arching, his muscles tensing. Ilaria was focused on the road, head down; she was right next to us, and Marco kept yelling and swerving toward her as if to bump against her. I held on to the edges of the rack. I didn't want to hold on to him. His scent grew stronger with every turn of the pedals. It was a scent I didn't recognize.

FOUR

GRANDMA ANNOUNCED THAT SHE WAS GOING TO
make me a dress. School will be starting again soon, she said.
You're growing up, right here, she said, running her hand
across her own chest, from left to right, as if she were tight-
ening an imaginary belt. She sewed as she watched TV in the
evening or sometimes in the afternoon after lunch, when it
was too hot to do chores. Every now and then she would look
up and stare at me, as if she were painting my portrait rather

than making me a dress. I knew she was trying to keep an eye on me. She looked only when she thought I wouldn't notice, but I did. Those days I kept catching her doing two things: watching me and rubbing her stomach. It must have been her colic again, and again she was trying to hide the pain from us, just as she had done all those years ago. Sometimes when we were sitting at the dinner table or out on the porch she would press her lips together and stand up very slowly to make her way back inside. She would emerge a few minutes later and head toward the vegetable garden or the stables, where I would hear her railing at the livestock or at the dogs, who kept getting tangled in her feet. Luna and Neve had made friends and went everywhere together now: if Luna got up, Neve would follow her, as if to copy her. I sat still and tried to work out how much time there was left before I would have to go back to school. Every morning when I woke up, the first thing I did was to count the days I had left, thinking that as long as I still had more than thirty to go, I didn't need to worry.

Ilaria and I were stretched out on the lawn one day, sunbathing in our swimsuits. We had two towels and a bottle of water between us, and whenever it got too hot, we would pour water over ourselves, rubbing it onto our arms and necks as if it were sunscreen. My grandma walked by and saw us.

"You'll get sunburn," she said. "You should cover your shoulders and chest at least. The sun is too hot at this time of day."

I turned to look at Ilaria and laughed, then lay back down on the grass. Soon after that, I realized that Grandma had gone.

That evening I saw the swarm for the first time. I was sitting on my bedroom floor, reading. I heard the noise through the open window. It was soft at first, a light, continuous hum that seemed to exist only in my ears. Soon it grew more distinct, like a murmuring buzz, forcing me to read the same sentence over and over, until I couldn't go on. I looked out the window, and in the saffron light of the lamp below I saw a soft black cloud, oscillating in the air like a soap bubble or a ghost. It was denser than the clouds of midges we were used to seeing in the summer and looked thick and heavy, like a mark made in ink instead of pencil. It moved quickly, blurring my vision. I squinted, trying to focus on one specific spot, and I realized it was a swarm of flies. I moved my head back, blinking. The cloud expanded, then contracted again. It drew shapes in the air—dogs, dragons, snakes. It made me think of those springtime afternoons when my father and I would lie down on the patch of daisies on our little hill and point out new shapes in the clouds every time they shifted. I watched the swarm until the shapes stopped making sense and it became impossible to tell which animal they looked like. The mosquito trap kept making short, sharp buzzing sounds, like a volley of bullets. Stupid creatures, I said to myself. It's a trap. There's nothing for you down there.

•

MY MOTHER HAD started working again. She'd found a job as a secretary at a real estate agent's office in the city. She came back late in the evenings, and sometimes she was too tired to even talk to us. She woke up early every day, had a shower, then spent almost an hour at the dressing table in her room, putting on her makeup and brushing her hair, which she'd started growing long, and which now had highlights. The makeup she put on her face covered the bags under her eyes, and the dresses she wore—short and brightly colored, with flowered patterns—made her seem younger. Of all my peers, I was the one whose mother was the youngest, a fact that was occasionally pointed out to me by my teachers or by the other girls in my class. She looks like your older sister, they would say. I couldn't see it. I wasn't even conscious of her beauty. I didn't notice it, I couldn't recognize it; it was not something I thought about when I looked at her. She was my mother, and that seemed to blur her outline and muddy her features for me. I understood that she was older than me, and that she was aging: I could see it in the photographs from when I was little, from before I was born. She was a different person now— I could see that, even though everyone kept telling her she still looked like a young woman. But even though it was not visible to my eyes, I was aware of her beauty. People still turned to look at her whenever we were in town together; I noticed every time it happened, though she didn't seem to. "Your mother was the most beautiful girl in school," my grandma used to tell me when I was little. "The most beautiful girl in town. She won a beauty pageant once. We were on holiday at the seaside with your grandfather and your aunts. She was sixteen. She was crowned 'Miss Summer 1982.' Her hair used to be very long back then, and wavy. She would wear it in a long plait down her back, like this, and then when she untied it, it came down in ripples, and she looked like a siren. There wasn't a single boy who wouldn't turn and stare when she walked by." She would tell me all these things within earshot of my father, who would look over at us, then walk away. Where did the crown go? I asked my grandmother. She shrugged and told me, "That's something only your mother knows. She's always been fond of keeping secrets."

The day after the flies, my mother came into my room without knocking. It was Sunday afternoon, so she wasn't at work, though she had taken the car out early in the morning and gone off somewhere with the excuse—supplied for my grandmother's benefit—that she needed to buy bread. Grandma and I were already at the table by the time my mother came back, bringing only three small bread rolls. "I looked all over the place for these," she said. "Everyone in the whole world must have gone out to buy bread this morning." I picked up a roll. It was crispy and covered with golden seeds, and smelled more strongly than the bread we usually ate. She must have bought it in the city, in one of those big shopping centers where you could buy all sorts of things, and where we went so rarely that it was like a special trip every time we did.

"Let's jump on the bed," she said, coming into my room and looking like she was in a rush. "Like we used to do when you were little, remember?" She grabbed my hand and pulled me up. "What were you doing on the floor?"

"Nothing," I said, trying to figure out if she was all right. Her cheeks were flushed and her eyes were moist. I thought she must have had an argument with Grandma, but I didn't ask.

She took off her shoes and climbed onto the bed. "Come on, Vale," she said. "I feel like dancing today!"

She took a few careful steps, her arms raised for balance. Then she pushed down with her toes, bent her knees, and started jumping, her hair following her movements, whirling in the air.

"Come on!" she said to me. She began to laugh. "What's that face for?" She stopped and reached toward me. "It's only me! Your mom, remember?" she said, still laughing, though this time it sounded forced. She had a beautiful laugh, anyway. I knew it must be one more thing about her that men went crazy for.

I decided to climb onto the bed, but I did not take her hand. I started jumping too, slowly at first, then higher, the bed creaking and crumpling beneath me with every leap, the air just about squeezing through my nose, as if I were submerged, the skin on my face lifting up and flopping down with the free fall.

My mother was the first to tire. "Enough. I'm out of breath. It was easier when you were little."

She sat down, her hair afloat, thin strands forming a little crown around her face. She took a deep breath, then threw herself backward onto the bed, her arms raised above her head as I looked down at her.

"It used to be a lot easier, I remember that. I think I've almost reached the age of exhaustion. It's getting closer." She smiled and closed her eyes.

I kept staring at her without even realizing I was doing it. She opened her eyes. "Do I look old to you?" she asked flatly.

I shook my head, then shook it again to get rid of the tor-
por that had come over me. I sat down beside her.

"Your grandma has a theory about wrinkles," she said.

We were lying down next to each other now, both staring
at the ceiling and its dark wooden beams converging into a
single point, up in the highest part of the roof. "What is it?"
I asked.

"She says every tear leaves a mark on your skin. Like a
river carving its course or a drop of water falling onto the
same spot every day. Do you remember that cave we went to
see? The one with the hole from that trickle of water?"

I told her I did remember. She'd taken me there a few
years before on one of our short holidays, a few days spent
together—just me, my mother, and my father—no farther
than a few hours' drive away. It was a chalk cave. It had none
of the stalactites and stalagmites I'd studied in school, only a
series of tunnels, some so low that my father had to crouch
down to make it through, but others big and round like the
mouth of a giant, with the air inside so cold that it hurt our
ears, and so humid that it seeped into our bones. Each of
these openings was known as a room, just as if it were part
of a house. And in fact the cave was like a house—a dark,
cold, abandoned house but a house nonetheless—and perhaps it had been used as one, thousands of years before we
had arrived. On top of one of these rooms was a round aper-
ture. It was quite narrow, and off on the side, but easy to spot
because it let in light, which then formed a circle on the floor,
like a spotlight. Through that hole came a trickle of water,
and that water had formed a pool in which the outside light

was reflected. It was a small hollow, limestone white, like an eye in the floor. The drip originated from a natural rainwater reservoir, which released a single drop of water every ten seconds, and had done so for thousands of years. The tour guide had called it "the power of slowness."

"Grandma thinks that wrinkles are the marks of the tears we shed," she said. "Why else, she says, would they form around our eyes and along the sides of our mouths, which is where tears run?"

She was silent for a moment before adding, "Of course it's bullshit. You can get wrinkles from laughing, too. Like this," she said, her face stretched into an exaggerated smile. "Or from concentrating. Or from worrying. See?" she said, frowning so her forehead wrinkled. "You can get loads of wrinkles here. But I know what to do: the trick is to make sure you feel no emotions at all. Remember, Vale. Never let any emotions in. Better start learning now. Getting old is so horrible," she said, clasping my hand and closing her eyes.

I looked at her now that she couldn't see me, and I remembered the story Grandma had told me. I had always wanted to ask her about it, and this seemed like the right moment. I called out to her: Mom. She groaned, her eyes still closed, as if to say, What now? Where's the crown? I asked. What crown? she said. The "Miss Summer 1982" one. She remained silent and still, forcing herself to keep her eyes closed—I was sure she wanted to open them—until she couldn't take it anymore. Grandma told you about that, didn't she? she asked, her tone more resigned than resentful.

I took in the sound of her breathing, and the scent of her

clothes. I felt like I hadn't smelled that scent in years. Then the buzzing returned. It was closer this time, and more defined. I turned around: my mother was staring at the ceiling with her eyes wide open and her brow furrowed, as if she'd been listening to the noise for a while. I gently freed myself from the grip of her hand, got up, and went toward the bathroom. The door was open. Inside the shower cubicle, through its transparent sides, I could see dozens of flies swirling like a black spiral, a vortex, contained within those glass walls but gathering in strength, charging, ready to escape, upward and out until it took over the whole house.

●

MARCO CAME BACK a few days later when we were on the lawn again, covered in sunscreen and water, which we occasionally poured over our heads and chest. We heard him calling out to us from a distance.

"I want a rematch," he yelled. "I've come for a rematch."

"Shhh," I said. "Who let you in?"

"Who do you think? Your grandma."

I looked behind him but couldn't see her.

"So? No dead weights this time, though," he said, smiling at me. "One person per bike, and you use your own."

"I don't want to," I said. "It's too hot."

"I don't want to either," said Ilaria. "Besides, I've already won."

"But the race was rigged!" he protested. "I know what it is: you're scared now."

Ilaria and I looked at each other and laughed. "We're never scared," she said.

"Let's go down to the river," I said.

"The river?"

"Yes. Let's show him what we found."

"What did you find?"

Ilaria smiled and narrowed her eyes. "What's the matter?" she said. "Are you scared now?"

•

THE RIVER WAS a stream two meters wide and a hand's breadth in depth, gurgling over dark, slippery rocks. Where the water was clear, you could see through to the bottom: tiny fish, algae, and water snakes. My father would take me there sometimes, and Ilaria, too. We'd remove our shoes so they wouldn't get wet, and pick our way barefoot across the mossy stones. He would hold our hands to make sure we didn't fall. When my father wasn't there, we went alone. One time we followed the river for quite a long way and we discovered a sort of clearing, a kind of pond where the water had settled and stagnated. The surface was covered with slime, a brilliant green so dense it looked like paint.

"Hurry up," I said to Marco. His progress over the rocks was slow. He was scared he might fall. "I can't believe you've never been here."

"You're such a sissy," Ilaria added.

He was taller than we were, and his steps were clumsy. He swayed from side to side, his shoes held in his outstretched hands. Ilaria and I knew where to plant our feet. We knew which rocks were safe and which were unstable, and we knew how to tell them apart. My father had led us over those paths before and shown us what to do.

We got to the pond eventually. The spell of dry weather had dimmed the greenness of the surface, and now it looked more like vegetable soup. Light filtered through the tree branches like the fingers of an enormous hand, and made the earth and all the invisible things that moved in the air glisten.

"What the hell is this?" he said from behind us. Ilaria and I were advancing at an almost identical pace. I turned around and realized he must be referring to the pond.

"Shut up!" I whispered, glaring at him. Our voices bounced among the boulders and the trees.

We made straight for the place we knew, our feet sinking into the soaked earth.

"Check this out," said Ilaria. "Let's see if you know what it is."

The strip of plastic was exactly where we'd last seen it. Among the leaves, in the rockiest spot. White as a dead fish.

"What?" he said.

"This," I replied, pointing.

He laughed. "Of course I know what it is."

"So say it," Ilaria insisted.

"It's a condom."

We all laughed, quietly.

"A used condom, to be precise."

He moved closer, studying it with an amused look on his face.

"Did one of you girls use it?"

Ilaria exhaled through her teeth. "As if! Idiot."

"Did you touch it?"

"Are you crazy?" I said. "We'd get diseases."

"I'll give you five thousand lire if you touch it."

"That's so gross," said Ilaria. "I would rather die."

"Cowards," he said. "So, is this it then?"

"No," said Ilaria. "There's something else."

She stepped past the strip of plastic, careful to avoid touching it even by mistake, then crouched down next to a rock.

"Cigarettes," she said.

"A full pack?"

"There's two here."

"Show me."

She lobbed them at him with a giggle, and he caught them—just about—with one hand.

"They're wet," he said. "We can't smoke them like this."

"We don't want to smoke them," said Ilaria.

"I do."

"Let's leave them out to dry," I said.

Ilaria glared at me.

"Just to give it a go," I continued.

"There's too much shade here," said Marco. "We should put them out in the sun."

We emerged from beneath the trees and started following the creek again. We climbed up the bank and soon found a clearing: yellow grass, a rusty tin-roofed shed, some abandoned tools scattered about.

"Let's find something to put them on," he said.

He found a large, flat rock and rested the cigarettes at opposite ends so they would dry quicker. We sat around the rock.

"Now what?" said Ilaria.

"Now we wait," said Marco.

"It'll take forever. I'm bored."

"Let's do something to pass the time."

"Like what?" I asked.

"Truth or dare," said Ilaria. "Do you know how to play?"

"Everyone knows how to play truth or dare," he replied.

The sounds of water and animals came from the creek. Insects. Birds. It felt like there was no one else around, no other human being, for miles. It felt like it had all been there since the beginning of time.

"You start. Truth or dare?"

"Why me?"

"Because you're outnumbered. So?"

"Truth."

The rock stood between us like a totem. Like a bonfire.

"What shall we ask him?" said Ilaria.

"I don't know," I said, looking at her. We thought about it for a while. She whispered something into my ear, and we both laughed. "Okay," I said.

"Have you ever kissed a girl?"

"Course," he said. "And not just one."

"I mean with your tongue."

"Sure."

"How many?"

"Six."

"Shut up."

"It's not my fault you're both such losers. I answered your question—now it's my turn. Ilaria, truth or dare?"

"Truth."

I checked the cigarettes. They were still wet. I turned them over, like meat on a grill.

"You have to tell us a secret. Something you've never told anyone else before."

"If I've never told anyone else before, I'm not going to tell you, am I?"

"It's the game. You have to do it."

She huffed. "Okay," she said, her eyes roaming about as she tried to think of something to say. "When I was little, I pinched my little brother's nose while he slept. I mean I pinched his nose and covered his mouth at the same time. I'd seen it in a film. He was like three months old, so he still slept in his crib. I wanted to see how long he'd last."

Marco burst out laughing. "So . . . you choked him?" he said. He rocked back and forth holding his stomach, his laugh echoing all around us. I was laughing, too.

"Did you really?" I said. "You never told me."

"You wanted to kill him," said Marco. "Tell the truth."

"No!" she said. "I mean, maybe. I don't know. I can't remember what I was thinking."

"Then what happened?"

"Then he woke up and started crying. My parents came in, and I acted like nothing had happened."

"Did they ever find out?"

"No. So if either of you ever says anything, I'll kill you."

We laughed again. Then Marco said, "Your turn."

"Vale, truth or dare?" said Ilaria.

"Dare," I said.

"Well, well, well!" said Marco.

"What shall we make her do?" asked Ilaria.

"It's up to you to decide. But I can give you tips," said Marco, winking.

"No," she said. "You have to kiss Marco. On the mouth."

"Bitch," I said.

Marco started making suggestive noises.

"Shut up," I said. "With or without tongue?"

"Oooh!" Ilaria screamed, pointing at me. "Did you hear that?"

"You'd love that, wouldn't you?" said Marco.

"I was only asking."

"No," said Ilaria. "No tongue."

"Thanks a lot," I said.

"Come on," said Marco, crossing his arms. "I'm ready."

I looked at him, and then I looked at Ilaria. I thought I'd get it over with quickly, and everything would be all right again. It wasn't so bad, and it was definitely better than the other option. We stood up. I leaned toward him and placed my lips against his. I had no idea where to put my hands.

"You jerk!" I said, pulling away. "She said no tongue!"

Marco snickered. "It must have come out by mistake."

"What an asshole," said Ilaria.

I wiped my lips on my sleeve. "That's gross."

"Yeah, right!" he said. "You loved it."

"I feel like I've just kissed my dog."

Ilaria laughed, and he did, too.

"So, what about these cigarettes?" said Marco.

"Let's see if we can smoke them anyway."

Marco picked one up and checked whether it was dry. "Where's the lighter?" he asked.

"We don't have one."

"Seriously?" he said.

"We thought you would," Ilaria needled him.

"That's actually why we brought you here in the first place."

"But we made a mistake," said Ilaria. "We thought you were smarter than this."

"Witches," he said. "You two are witches."

"Now we'll have to kill you," Ilaria went on.

"I'm so scared," he said.

I thought I could hear the buzzing of the flies. "I'll sneak one off my mother," I said.

"Your mother," said Marco. "Can I come say hello to your mother, too?"

"Do you know her?"

"Of course I do. Everyone knows her."

I looked him right in the eye and leaned forward, silently daring him to keep talking. Suddenly I wasn't afraid anymore. I felt like I'd known him forever, like we'd been there before.

"Your mother is smoking hot."

"Shut up," I said. I could feel the fury rising from my belly all the way up to my chest.

"What?" he said. "I wouldn't mind having my way with her."

I went right up to him and grabbed his shirt. I wanted to

punch him in the face, to wipe that filthy smirk off his face. Perhaps I would have done it, if Ilaria hadn't intervened.

"Both of you stop it," she said. She grabbed my arm. "Come on, let him be. You're not about to get into a fight like some boy, are you?"

"I'm not scared of her," said Marco.

I let go of his shirt, but I shoved him first. One hand on his shoulder and the other, a fist, on his chest. I managed to shift him by a few inches, and he had to shuffle backward to stay on his feet. The two of them were staring at me now, open-mouthed. I had no idea what had gotten into me.

I turned around and started walking back home. I could still feel a heat in my stomach, around my neck, inside my throat. A savage, I kept telling myself. If your grandmother could see you, she would say you're a savage. And yet I felt proud of what I'd done. If I'd pushed any harder, I would have made him fall.

He caught up with me soon after that—perhaps Ilaria had suggested it. He shouted out my name first, then ran to make up the ground.

"I'm sorry," he said. "I didn't mean to make you angry."

Though I was practically over it already, I let myself sulk for a while longer, just like my mother did with me whenever I did something wrong. I let him make the effort to persuade me. And he did—he made the effort. I liked the feeling that gave me. I had the very clear sensation of being bigger than him, of having him in my grasp: it was like I had him on a leash and was letting him thrash about. It was like those moments just before I started squeezing the frogs between my fingers.

I made him say, "I liked what we did earlier." Then I persuaded him to look at me, to reach out for me again. I had watched my mother do the same to my father years ago. I pulled back when I saw that Ilaria was about to catch up with us. We dropped Marco home first, and then Ilaria walked me back so she could pick up her bike. We went slowly, pausing every few feet; we didn't feel like going home. When I got back, it was nighttime. I'd almost forgotten about the flies, the mosquitoes, what had come before, and what some part of me was sure would come again. I had almost forgotten about Neve, about my mother, my grandmother, my father. It's crazy how quickly you can forget things when you are little, when you still have some trust left, and the effect it has when you discover that everything is still exactly where you had left it, waiting for you.

My mother and grandmother were in the kitchen, throwing food away. The cupboards were all open, letting out flies in thick, droning clusters.

"Jesus Christ," my mother was saying. "What's happening to this house?"

The food in the bin was crawling with maggots. Neve kept trying to look. She wanted to see.

"Take her away," Grandma said. "Take her outside."

"And stay outside with her," my mom said. "This place is disgusting."

"What's happening?" I asked.

"We have to clean the fridge out," said my mother. "It looks like everything in there is rotting."

My grandmother corrected her: "We have to clean the whole kitchen out."

"Where are they coming from?" said my mother. She kept staring at the cupboards. "Where the hell are they coming from?"

"I told you," said my grandma. "I told you to be careful. I always tell you, but it's never enough with you. What do I have to do for you to listen?"

FIVE

I STARTED GOING OVER TO MARCO'S HOUSE EVEN
when Ilaria was not around. I didn't tell her about it, but I
didn't ask him to keep it secret either; Marco didn't know she
would be upset if she found out. When Ilaria and I were alone
together, we always talked about him. We talked about him
for hours: we both liked him, and I began to leave out some of
the details only I knew or that I was gradually discovering—
about the way his bedroom looked, about his parents, about

the strawberry-colored birthmark on his chest—so that she would not think either of us had any advantage over the other, so that she would be sure neither of us ever would, because our friendship was more important than anything.

I would go to his house in secret and tell him that we could kiss, but only in there, and that outside we would have to act as if there were nothing going on. I didn't tell him about Ilaria. I just hoped she would never find out; it was one of the things I prayed for every night. At some point I made a list of all the things I was praying for—I'm sure it was there in my mind for a time, each plea corresponding to a number. A list of all the things that no one else must ever know and that I kept burying deeper and deeper, one on top of another, hoping the stack would never get so tall as to reveal itself. The truth is that even though every secret carries its own measure of filth, that very filth soon becomes irresistible, until you can never have enough. It may sound absurd, but I think it must be because that is how we try to remove it every time: by adding more and more, until there's too much of it there to hide—though by the time you realize that, it's far too late. You don't know that when you're in the midst of it all, no matter what the Bible teaches, no matter what your parents tell you about the importance of truth and prevention. You don't know that when you're in the midst of it all, and especially if you're twelve years old. So I kept quiet about the blood, and about Marco, and about anything else I could possibly keep quiet about. And I kept touching myself—at night, during the day, whenever, really—without even closing my bedroom door, wondering all the while whether Ilaria did it too, if she had ever done it before, and hoping that someday soon the priest would ask me about it during confession so that I could tell him no.

I would go over to Marco's, covering the distance between my house and his in long strides, sometimes running all the way so that the effort and the heat would stop me from having to think about the tension I felt in my stomach on the way there and the guilt on my shoulders on the way back. Only when I got to his place and he came to the door to let me in, keeping me waiting for a minute or two as if he always had more important things to do, only when I stepped into that empty house with its pleasant smell and its vast array of white ornaments that looked like they might topple over if you stared at them for too long, only then did I let myself breathe—like when you're playing a game of hide-and-seek and you manage to make it safely back to home base. We would sit on the living room carpet, where we would talk without looking at each other, and though I think we could both feel there was an emptiness there, we kept doing it anyway because we craved that emptiness, like some unpleasant thing you slowly get used to until you can no longer live without it.

We would watch a movie or maybe some music videos on TV, and when it was almost time for dinner, almost time for me to leave, we would start kissing. We would keep our distance, fingers skimming over each other's shoulders, arms, and hands; sometimes he would hold my hips and I would wish he would go further. When I was alone at night, in the dark, I would think back to those moments and hope that the next time his hands might brush over my breasts and my thighs, creep past the waistline of my trousers, with his mother likely to come home at any moment. But when we were together, I was scared. As soon as we heard the key turning in the lock, and sometimes even sooner, we would spring away from each other and I would tiptoe out of the house before Marco's mother could see me. I didn't like his mother. She always looked like she had better things to do than to deal with you or listen to anything you had to say, even if the only words coming out of your mouth were answers to some polite inquiry ("How is your mother?" or "Are you sure you don't want to stay for dinner?"), which, in spite of everything, she would always be sure to make. She meted out the same treatment to Marco's father—a tall man with a shrill voice, bright eyes, and emphatic mannerisms who wore light gray or sand-colored trousers held up by suspenders that made his appearance even more awkward, as if he were a character in a sitcom whose job was to get a laugh out of the audience every time he came home, and who always managed to put me at ease. He could make anyone laugh—anyone except Marco's mother, who would look at him as if she'd had enough of his ways, as if she already knew what he was about to say and so no longer found it amusing.

But with Marco, she was tremendously affectionate. As soon as she walked in, and no matter what we were doing, Marco would stand up and run to greet her, perhaps with a peck on the cheek, and to relieve her of her shopping bags. She would kiss him too, then disappear for a few minutes before returning to gather him in a tight embrace, as if he were still a child. He would protest and try to wriggle away, and she would tease him. Then she would start tidying up his room or making dinner. She would call him "sweet-heart" and "darling," but while my mother only ever used those kinds of words when she was in a playful mood or trying to make amends for something, and even then only in an ironic falsetto, Marco's mother did it naturally, in the manner of someone who said that kind of thing as a matter of course. I thought this must be the way people treated their male offspring.

When Marco and I kissed, glued to each other for ages, my mind would begin to wander. My mother, my father, Neve, the frogs and the insects, all of it running through my mind as if I were on the verge of death. Memories would come to me like electrical impulses, and I found I could neither control nor arrange them—so I let them do as they willed. There was one scene in particular that recurred quite frequently. My mother, knocking one of my grandmother's decorative objects over while doing the dusting—on one of those rare occasions when she decides to perform the chore of her own volition and without complaint. She knocks over a painted clay figurine— probably a saint, though I do not recall which one, and per-haps I never knew to begin with. She begs me: Please, please, can you tell her it was you? She won't say anything if she thinks it was you. I tell her, No, please no. I am terrified. I don't want to take the blame for something I didn't do. Grandma will be angry. She was fond of that figurine. I don't want to take the blame. Please, she says. Do it for me. Don't you love me? Do it for me. I'm begging you. She won't be angry. I relent, and Grandma punishes me by banishing me to my room. My mother comes in to bring me my dinner. You were very brave, she says. I'm proud of you. She has hidden a piece of chocolate in the tray. I cry as I eat it. Once the taste has faded, I dry my tears. I am proud of myself.

•

MY MOTHER HAD been giving me freer rein recently, and asking me fewer questions. Grandma had been trying to do the same, trying not to meddle, but every time I came home she would still ask me where I'd been. At Ilaria's, I would reply, and she would let me in with nothing more than a wordless look, leaving me with the illusion that I had gotten away with it—even though every time she looked at me like that, in silence, her head leaning slightly to one side, I was convinced she could read my mind.

At dinner one night my mother had still not come home from work and Grandma scolded me for handling my fork wrong.

"You're holding it like a dog would. The Lord gave you hands," she said. "Not paws. Look," she said, demonstrating the correct way, holding her fork near the tip of its handle between her finger and thumb.

I scoffed. Grandma gave me a stern look, the kind I thought she must so often have turned on her daughter too, but that my mother had only rarely managed to replicate.

"You mustn't let anyone think we are country people. We might live here, but we are not hicks. If your grandfather were still with us, we would have better things to do with our time than to deal with the mud and the beasts and all the rest of it.

THE EMPIRE OF DIRT 85

Mold and dust, too. Never forget: the things that you do determine the way people think of you," she said. "The details. The devil's in the details. Remember that."

She lifted the napkin from her lap to wipe her mouth, then took a sip of red wine, draining the glass. She poured out some more. The bottle, made of dull green glass, with a plastic stopper on top and no label, was one of Enzo's. He must have dropped in earlier that day to bring some more. He came more often now that my father was gone. I think he must have felt it was his duty.

"The devil," she went on. "He sees everything, just like the Lord does."

She kept eating her food, in small, slow mouthfuls. Her eyes were on her plate, but I knew that they would soon be fixed on me again.

"Your grandfather would know what to do. He'd know what to do about the animals."

"The animals?" I asked.

"The sheep," she clarified. "They're sick."

"What's wrong with them?"

She passed the napkin over her mouth again. "Enzo is the one who pointed it out. They're lying on the ground, not moving," she said, and smiled. It was odd of her to do that. She shook her head. "Their tongues have gone black. Your grandfather's tongue was always black. And he always smelled of licorice. Licorice killed your grandfather. Licorice and cigarettes."

She pushed her chair back and stood up, leaning silently on the table with her withered hands.

"So now it is the turn of the beasts," she whispered. "Do you know what's next?"

I looked at her, hoping she'd continue. She didn't. So I shook my head.

"Read the Book of Exodus," she said. "Read it again and again until you've learned it all by heart."

•

THE NEXT DAY I followed Grandma to the enclosure where the sheep were. Two had already died, and several others could no longer stand. Their muzzles had swollen up, as if they'd been kicked and beaten.

We called the veterinarian. My mother kept staring at the dead sheep, making sure to stand outside the enclosure. She decided to call my grandfather, too—my father's father—even though he was retired. "It's always best to have a second opinion," she said.

My grandfather was a tall man with gray whiskers and long, deep-set eyes that were always narrowed, open only as much as they had to be for him to be able to see. He rarely smiled, and only out of politeness—a quick greeting when he saw me—and every time he looked at me, I feared that he might scold me. He had broad shoulders and a bloated, protruding belly, and he did not look like my father. His wife, my grandmother, had an illness that meant she couldn't leave the house on her own or move at all without falling over.

He got there before the new veterinarian did. He told us

it was bluetongue disease, and that it was contagious. "You'll need to report the outbreak," he said.

I wanted to ask him if it could infect humans too, but I didn't dare. I hoped someone else would, and eventually my mother did.

"Should we keep our distance? Are we at risk?" she asked.

He shook his head. "It only affects animals. Transmitted by insect bites. Sheep, goats, livestock. But it's sheep that are most affected. You may have to put them down," he said.

The new veterinarian arrived and confirmed the diagnosis. He checked the other animals and said they seemed fine. "But we will have to run some tests. And report the outbreak. Keep the other beasts away from the sheep."

"Can it be treated?" asked Grandma.

The veterinarian said no. Grandma shook her head. "Not at all?" she asked. "I'm sorry," said the veterinarian.

Grandma said no more. My mother took me back up to the house. I kept asking why we had to kill them all, even the ones that weren't sick. I started crying: I didn't want to, but I couldn't stop.

A few days later, the test results came back. Some of the sheep had deteriorated, and the two that had already been unable to move had since died. Enzo came by every day to change their hay, give them their medicine, and take away the ones that had died. The day they came to put the sheep down, I stayed in my room and watched through the window as the veterinarian arrived. I watched him for as long as I could. I was a little wary of going downstairs because I knew that if my grandmother or my mother caught me, they would send me straight back up, but I told myself I must be strong and go and see what was about to happen. It was no more than I deserved. So I went out and approached the sheep pen from the back, through the orchard. I hid among the trees, lying flat on my stomach so I could see better. The sheep were thrashing their legs, and their wails sounded like the crying of newborn babies. They were being led away one at a time: it took at least two people to hold them still, and sometimes my grandma or Enzo had to help, too. My mother would go to the ones that seemed most restless, bend down to look them in the eyes, and say: Don't worry, don't worry.

I ran back into the house. All I wanted was to get back into bed and stay there forever. I went past my grandmother's room and saw her bottle of holy water. I rubbed at my eyes to get rid of the tears that were still stuck there, obscuring my vision even after all that running, and I went inside. The bottle stood on her dressing table; it was made of plastic and shaped like the Madonna. She must have brought it back from Lourdes or Medjugorje or one of those places to which the parish arranged trips every now and then, and where she would go so that she could pray for us. The Madonna was tall and slender and white—white like the lace doily she stood on, which my grandmother had made to cover the dressing table. The Madonna's hands rested on her belly, where Jesus was, and over her belly hung a ribbon, blue like the crown that rested on her head and that was, in fact, the cap that secured the holy water inside her. I pulled the cap off, though it took me a while, as it had been sealed so that no water would leak out during the journey. I had to twist hard and use the hem of my T-shirt for a better grip. Finally the cap gave way. I brought the bottle to my lips and drank a sip—a small one, so that Grandma wouldn't notice the difference. The water tasted of old plastic and I almost spat it back out, but I resisted the urge and swallowed instead. Then I put the bottle back in its place and went up to my room, back to bed. I could still feel the water in my throat and in my chest, down in my stomach, as if it had carved out a track that would never go away. I fell asleep without realizing it.

I dreamed that the sheep had come inside and were watching me from the corridor. I could see their heads as if they were standing right in front of me. I dreamed that their tongues had gone blue, just like mine would do in the summer when I had too many aniseed ice pops. Their eyes were also blue. Their bodies were the same color as the bottle shaped like the Madonna. I dreamed that I stole the bottle: I took it to my room and put it on my bedside table, and the sheep wouldn't leave until I drank it. I dreamed that the water was poisoned and made my heart explode.

In some other place, in some other time, my father wakes up when he hears me screaming.

In some other time, in some other place, my father bundles me up in his arms and holds me until the rest of the dream has faded away.

BLUE

IN TOWN, THERE WAS ONLY ONE OF EVERY KIND OF shop. One café, one greengrocer, one butcher, one baker. The only exception were the two diners, which had always coexisted peacefully; they received their supplies of eggs, fruits, and vegetables from us. There was also a little supermarket now where the old convenience store used to be; I still remembered that store for its overwhelming smell of newspapers, even in the refrigerated section, where the milk and cheese were kept.

Now the newspapers had been moved to a smaller room, but the owner had not lost his habit of stocking all kinds of other wares, from beach accessories to beauty products.

I was out shopping with my grandmother when I saw the spray cans. The newsagent had put them near the hair dyes Grandma used to buy when she wanted to avoid the hairdresser—she used to hate going to the salon, thought it was a waste of time. But by now her hair had gone almost completely white, each strand as thick as a post, and it would morph into all kinds of strange shapes if she forgot to get it trimmed regularly. The spray cans looked like the kind people used to draw graffiti (I knew what those looked like from seeing them in movies), but the description said they were for hair. The label read: *Hair spray— temporary hair dye—will last until your next wash.* The color could be worked out from the round sticker affixed to the lid: pink, orange, purple, green, blue. Grandma was talking to the newsagent—he'd found out about the sheep and wanted to know if the disease was infectious—and I stood there examining the cans until she called me over. We went on to the supermarket and I looked in there too, down the aisle with all the hair-care products, but couldn't see any there.

I told Ilaria about it the next day. I was sure she'd never seen the cans before.

"Let's get some," she exclaimed. "How much are they?"

"Eleven thousand lire."

"That's expensive. My mom will never let me take that much."

"We could get one and share it. Five thousand, five hundred lire each."

"Will it be enough for both?"

"Maybe. We could spray a little each in turns until we run out. What color do you want?"

"Pink," said Ilaria. "Or purple. I don't know. What do you think would be prettiest?"

"Blue. I'd say blue."

"God no! We'd look like Smurfs. Pink would look cuter."

"Yes, but do you remember the siren in that book of fairy tales we used to read in primary school? Do you remember she had blue hair, and we said that when we grew up we'd have blue hair, too? And it's cooler than pink anyway. Pink is for posers. We'd look like we had icing sugar on our heads."

It took me another five minutes to persuade Ilaria, but she finally agreed. I always managed to convince her in the end, even if she always grumbled to begin with. Now we had to do the same with our mothers. Our one advantage was that it was a washable dye that would come off with one shampoo, and that was the detail we decided to focus on.

We were sitting on a bench in the only children's playground in town. Two swings, one slide, and a few spring rockers for younger kids. They were usually brought there to play in the early evenings, when the air was cooler. But right then, just after lunchtime, the park was deserted. The swings stood motionless in the dense summer heat, their black plastic seats seemingly melting in the sun, wrinkled and formless like discarded chewing gum, and tarnished by years of wear and by children's hands.

Marco met us there. He arrived on his bike and put it next to ours; he could recognize them by now. He sat beside us, perching on the back edge of the bench, and began, in his own way, to tease us.

"Why don't you kiss, then?" he said when he noticed that Ilaria and I were holding hands.

I remembered the hair dyes, and suddenly I had an idea. "We'll do it if you give us eleven thousand lire."

Marco laughed. "Why eleven?"

"Because that's what we need."

"What for?"

"None of your business."

"Then I won't give it to you."

"We need to dye our hair," said Ilaria.

"But that's beside the point anyway. It's a bet. Take it or leave it."

"You wouldn't dare. I meant kissing with tongue, obviously."

"Try us," I said. "The money first."

He stared at me, trying to work out if I was being serious. I had no idea how I managed to hold his gaze. Every time I looked him in the eyes I was struck by how beautiful and fierce he seemed. It was a feeling I would never fully understand, so irritating that it made me want to hurt him—part of me would have liked to push him over, punch him in the face, on that white and perfect nose of his—and it turned something inside me into liquid. Until finally, by some strange process taking place inside my body, the attraction became synthesized and transfigured into rancor, a kind of irksome disdain that made me behave more aggressively than I otherwise would have. I think that was the first time it happened—not necessarily the first time I noticed it, but perhaps the first time I felt that small, subterranean wave of hatred it came with.

He laughed, displaying a row of small, straight, proud teeth, forged by a set of recently removed braces. He dug through his pockets and extracted a handful of crumpled banknotes. It was more than Ilaria and I had been able to set aside, and almost as much as the money our parents kept in their wallets. "Right, here it is. Now it's your turn."

I looked at Ilaria to see if she was game. She showed no signs of hesitation. Everything happened very quickly; I don't even remember who leaned in first. We cradled each other's head, hands on the back of each other's neck and in each other's hair, like we'd seen in the movies. We wanted to—both of us wanted to, I think—give the impression that we would laugh if we could. As if to say, This is just a dare. There's nothing in this we're actually enjoying; we're doing it for your eyes only, just to show you that we can.

We pressed into each other, mouths open, making our tongues touch. I felt nothing. It was only her; I knew her well, I knew her smell. It was as if we'd been doing it forever. It was not like kissing Marco, when my body would react as if to an invasion, to a virus or a foreign body, to a blast of antibodies. We clung on for another moment, then sprang apart and burst out laughing. Marco said, "Is that it?," then laughed to hide his embarrassment and complained that he would have liked to see more, though we refused. He kept laughing, taunting us, convinced that he had the upper hand, but I knew that he was the one who needed to defend himself: I could sense it, as if he had suddenly become a minuscule thing before us, two shadows growing larger and larger with every snicker.

•

MY MOTHER HAD now entered into a phase of rebellion against my grandmother. She seemed to want to force her way back to a state of adolescence she had never properly experienced, back to an epoch of her life she had rushed through, until it had slipped away from right under her nose—just as she was beginning to realize that she might do something with it. The way she manifested this now was by allowing me to do things Grandma forbade. So I knew there would be no trouble, and indeed she thought it was a splendid idea.

"Do they really sell hair dye like that now? In spray cans, like paint? That's marvelous. I'll come with you when you buy it—I want to see what they're like."

"Will Grandma be fine with it?"

She scoffed. "Oh, I can decide for you. If she doesn't like it, she'll just have to live with it."

"Of course she won't like it. She's a pain in the ass."

Her expression changed. "Don't ever say that again. Don't talk about your grandmother that way."

"But that's what I think," I objected. "And so do you."

Her eyes were serious now, wide open. Hard like Grandma's. It was almost scary.

"She's my mother. She's your grandmother," she said, reining her words in. "She has done so much for us, and still does. She loves us. And she wasn't always like this. You know that."

I thought about that later. Some part of me knew it was true, but I had begun to forget. I wondered if I'd begun to forget my father, too. I tried to recall his voice, his face. I tried to remember the way his face looked when he was eating, or when he took me somewhere, just the two of us.

I decided it was my mother's responsibility to talk to Grandma about the hair dye; if she didn't, then I wouldn't either.

I bought the can with Ilaria one afternoon. I didn't want my mother to be there; it was our business and no one else's. I remember it as one of the first things I ever bought with my own money, and certainly the very first thing I bought with money I had earned. How I'd earned it—through a dare or through work—didn't matter much. The important thing was that it had not been given to me by my grandmother or by my father just because I was their granddaughter or daughter. I had earned that money through something I had done.

We dyed our hair in Ilaria's bathroom one day when her parents were at work, so that my grandmother wouldn't see us until we had finished the job, by which time it would be too late for her to stop us and she would have no choice but to accept the fact, swallow it, and wait until a shower washed it all off. We followed the instructions on the can, shaking it first and holding it four inches away from our hair before we sprayed, taking care to aim the jet properly so that we didn't get any on the tiles; it hadn't been difficult to persuade Ilaria's mother to give us permission, but she would have killed

us if we'd gotten so much as a single stray speck of blue anywhere. The spray can caused an infernal racket and stink, but
I enjoyed the noise. We took it in turns to spray its contents
on each other's head, little by little so as to calibrate the color
properly. But we ran out anyway, sooner than expected, too,
and the result was that we both ended up with mottled hair,
the coloring more uniform near the backs of our necks but
with hardly any around the temples, while on Ilaria's dark
hair, the blue dye assumed a greenish hue, like oxidized copper. "We look like we've got some kind of disease," she said
as we studied ourselves in the mirror, and burst into raucous
laughter. The color stood out more on lighter hair, bleached
after months of sunshine. I held up one of my own locks for a
closer look; by now my hair had grown long enough to reach
my nipples, and when I was naked and about to have a bath,
I would amuse myself by draping it over my breasts—which
were still not as fully formed as my mother's or even like Ilaria's were, the way I yearned for mine to be every time I looked
at them. I would gather my hair into two wet strands and flip
them forward to see how much of my body they would cover,
like some tribeswoman or sea creature. I would sit in the hot
bath and examine my still-hollow chest, not so different from
the way it had looked a few years or a few months before,
"nothing to report," as I had once overheard my mother tell
my grandmother when they were talking about me, both of
them wondering when I would become a woman while thinking I was still a child—and that thought, that hidden crack
that ran between us, made me feel good.

The reactions to our blue hair were: dismay from Ilaria's mother, who marched her straight back to the bathroom and made her wash it off. ("That's disgusting—it looks like your head is rotting.") It took only a minute for the blue to spew back out, in contrast to the thirty minutes we had spent getting it out of the can and spreading it carefully over her hair—an outcome that did no justice to our efforts. Then: wry enjoyment from Ilaria's brother, who laughed through the entire rinsing operation. Finally: indifference from her father, who got home only after his daughter's hair had already been washed and dried, and could therefore witness the dye's effects only on me. He did examine some of my lighter locks under a lamp, though, as if he were studying some alien life-form, his manner a mixture of curiosity and revulsion, and he also checked to make sure there were no traces of the color left on his daughter. There weren't.

I went home feeling different. I could still smell the spray, and it was irresistible; I kept pulling locks of my hair down to my nose and leaving it there, held in place by my upper lip. My mother was the first to see me when I arrived, and she burst out laughing at the sight. She came over to examine my hair. "Oh God," she said. "It looks like someone's thrown up on you."

Then she laughed again and patted my head. "It would have come out better if you'd used the whole can. Look at this one," she said, picking out one of the bluer locks. "It's a pretty color. It complements your eyes."

She turned away. "Grandma's in, too. Go and show yourself."

Grandma was sitting on the rocking chair on the porch.

It was not often that I saw her sitting down before dinner. She was rocking and staring into the distance.

"Grandma, look. But don't worry, it comes off with shampoo."

Grandma barely turned her head. It seemed like she couldn't shake off her thoughts. She furrowed her brows, but it was a while before she said anything.

"Blue," she said. "It's blue."

"It washes off," I said. "It's not forever."

"You did it because of me, didn't you? You did it because you think it's my fault."

I stared at her. All of a sudden, she seemed hideously ugly.

"Stop it," I said. "Stop talking that way."

My mother appeared. "Don't shout," she said. "Grandma's tired."

"So am I," I said. "I don't want to be here anymore."

I ran toward the stables, toward the fences. It was already dark. I went where the sheep used to be. Everything was still and silent. I stopped with my belly pressed against the fence. I could feel the wood against my intestines, hard against my hips; I could hear my own breathing, the accelerated beat of my heart. It's not my fault, I told myself. It's not my fault.

SIX

THERE WAS AN ALBINO FAMILY LIVING IN TOWN. The mother and her three kids, two girls and one boy who were all older than me, would walk around like elves, their heads always covered up in the summer to make sure they didn't get sunburned. One day when I was still little, my mother explained what albinism was; before that, I had always just thought of them as being incredibly blond.

"Can you see their eyelashes?" she said. "They're white.

And their eyes seem blank. Or red, if you look closer. They can't see as well as we do. And they can't be out in the sun, or they'll get burned."

"Like vampires," I said.

"Like vampires," my mother echoed. "Your grandmother actually believes that, you know. She says that back in her day it was a mark of the devil. When their daughter was born— they named her Bianca; now, you tell me if that's not a little cruel—it was the first time anything like it had ever happened around here. The parents are old now and their hair is white too, but when they were younger it was darker than dark, and they were always so tanned. But even so that girl came out this way—bleached. Your grandma says that when the priest found out, he went to bless the house. Keep in mind this was in the sixties, not the Middle Ages. Anyway, it took a while to figure out that she was an albino. Rumor has it the father threatened to leave. He thought the child wasn't his."

"Why was she born that way?" I asked.

"I don't know. It's something in the genes."

"I think they're beautiful," I said.

"They are," she said, nodding. "And they shouldn't be living here. People here are stupid, much too stupid. *They* belong in another world."

We used to see them in church every Sunday. They would sit on the raised step in the last row, but right at the very end of the pew, so that while some of them remained in the shadows, others were illuminated by the light coming in through the church window, creating a portrait of pristine purity and celestial radiance that I was sure they wouldn't have chosen.

The mother always wore black or gray, and a hat she kept on throughout the service (Grandma had once told me that it was allowed, but only for women), while the girls wore pastel-colored gowns—teal, turquoise, or indigo—that went all the way to the floor in winter and just below the knee in summer. For the boy, who was the youngest, raw-cotton suits—navy or baby blue—and a pale shirt. The father always wore a good suit, always the same starched dark gray jacket and trousers, and followed his wife and children from a few steps behind, as if to protect them or to admire their cruel, defiant, desperate beauty—something that he was still not accustomed to, something that he had not been given access to, and that he would never accept or truly understand.

As they grew older, the middle child—the younger of the two daughters (I either did not know or could not remember their names, a fact that only enhanced their splendor in my eyes)—tried to rebel against her genes and against fate itself. She was five or six years older than me, and when I was still in primary school, she started attending high school in the city. She started wearing makeup on her eyes, her eyelashes, and later began to dye her hair black—a color that ended up looking more like blue on her and always faded too quickly, revealing what she was trying to hide. She wore jeans ripped at the knees, thick sweaters, loud earrings, colorful hats. She would show up at church like that on Sundays, and when she walked in my grandma would always look at her with her lips pressed tight together and her eyebrows arched. Eventually the girl stopped coming to church altogether. She also stopped coming home. One day, she simply never came home from school.

She was sixteen when she disappeared. I found out then that she was called Greta. For months her name and an old photograph where she was not smiling but staring straight at the camera, her eyes blank, were shown on television and published in the newspapers, the black-and-white print making it seem like she was even farther away, like she had never even existed. Grandma stopped buying the newspaper and also forbade me from reading it.

Every now and then my mother would say, "She'll come back, you'll see. It's not as if she's been kidnapped. She just went down the wrong path, that's all. And unless she's still on it, she'll come back."

"What if she doesn't?" I would ask.

"Trust me," she'd reply. "I know how these things go."

So did my grandmother, who had stopped watching the news and had begun kneading her stomach again. "I should pay her mother a visit," she'd say, shaking her head. "Poor woman."

"She was always the weakest, their middle child," my mother would say. "It was obvious. They should have thought about it sooner."

This would anger my grandmother: "It's not their fault. Don't you dare say anything like that again."

Then Greta returned. People were already talking about it before anyone even saw her. For weeks, for months, she didn't leave their house. We crossed paths at the supermarket one day when I'd gone into town with Grandma, and I recognized her by her hair. I was eleven, she was seventeen; it was the spring of 1995, the year before all that was going to happen had started to happen. Her hair, so blond it was almost white, the same hair she'd never let show for more than a couple of centimeters at the roots ever since she'd first begun to hide it, had now grown at least a hand's width above the fading dye. It reached all the way to her shoulders in a messy cut her mother must have given her, and it was tousled, as if she hadn't combed it once since I had last seen her. The two-tone effect, with the tips a different color from the top of her head, made her look like a silver fox. Her eyes looked even lighter, and they seemed to stand still even when they moved, so that she looked more sorrowful and more beautiful than ever before. I stopped and stared at her until Grandma shook me and dragged me away, but I could have stood watching her for hours and she wouldn't have noticed. She was in the toiletries aisle, picking a deodorant or perhaps a pack of sanitary pads. I didn't really take much notice; none of that meant anything to me at the time.

She left again after a few months, this time with the rest of her family, too. They moved to the city, to some suburban neighborhood where they were able to find a new, inexpensive home.

•

WHEN THE BOILS started to appear and I realized the sun made them worse, I thought of the albino family. I remembered their white skin, as delicate as old peoples', like papier-mâché. I stopped sunbathing and wearing tank tops. I picked out looser clothing, long sleeves, a tunic I'd found in my mother's wardrobe and had taken to wearing, unbeknownst to her, when she wasn't in. I told Ilaria I had a sunburn from sunbathing in the middle of the day, and that way I was able to stay in the shade, all covered up, while she lay on the lounger or on the grass, letting the sun warm her through, the tan lines from her swimsuit growing increasingly marked. Mine, too, were still there: I would check them every evening in front of the bathroom mirror, and think of when my skin would go back to being pale, and thin, and smooth again, like the whites of a hard-boiled egg.

The boils had come at night, like the blood. I woke up one morning and there they were, on my chest and my shoulders. It was just a few small red dots at first. But over the next few days they began to grow and swell, and soon they spread to my face, to my chin and forehead. I had read in one of those magazines for teenaged girls that Ilaria and I used to buy at the newsstand in town that it was common for pimples to appear with the onset of puberty. But I knew these weren't pimples; they were boils. I knew this because that night I had dreamed of a dust storm. I was reading the Book of Exodus every day, like Grandma had told me to do. I read it right before going to sleep at night and as soon as I woke up in the morning. I read it without telling my mother about it. I read it, and in it I found everything that was happening and that had already happened, and I prayed for it all to stop, because I knew what was yet to come.

I kept a close watch, during those days, for any marks that might also appear on my mother and grandmother. I tried to spy on them from different rooms in the house, studying them as they went about their tiniest moments, while they cooked or tidied up or fixed their hair in front of the mirror. I kept waiting for them to do something—to scratch themselves, to roll up their sleeves, lift up the hem of their dress, search their own skin with their fingertips. I waited secretly, patiently, and when I noticed, after two days, a mark on my mother's wrist—like a mosquito bite but bigger and redder—I convinced myself that it was a boil, and that made me feel less alone. I hoped I would see some on Grandma, too; I convinced myself I could see them. I didn't want to protect them anymore; I wanted this to be something I shared with them. I wanted them beside me. It was a road too dark to walk alone.

•

I DECIDED TO stay out of Ilaria's sight, and to never leave my room if I could help it. It was hard to hide the blemishes on my face, but in my mother's makeup kit I had found a biscuit-colored powder that—when carefully applied— seemed to work. After lunch, when Grandma slept and Mom went to work, I would go to the stables, to the enclosure where the goats, the chickens, and the ducks were kept; I would peer into the rabbits' cages and check each and every animal, one by one. I knew it would be their turn soon. Goats and cows often carried scars, dark grooves that looked like burns. They gave each other these scars when they fought or inflicted them upon themselves when they banged into the fence or rubbed themselves against it. Grandma had told me about it, but I also saw it happen with my own eyes every time a scuffle broke out between two goats or every time one of them went up to the fence and started scratching itself against it, so hard and for so long that sometimes blood came out. I would always stand and watch, so that I could see how far they would go. It was as if they couldn't feel any pain, or perhaps they enjoyed it. The goats always closed their eyes when they did this, but when they sensed my presence they would step away from the fence and turn to look at me. Sometimes they would come toward me so that I would pet them. I liked goats; they had melancholy, meaningful expressions, more so than Grandma's dog, who always looked a little dazed. They also had a very pronounced scent that stuck to your hands even if you washed them afterward, and to your clothes. Sometimes I would give the youngest ones— those that had just been weaned—one of my fingers to suckle on. I had learned how not to get bitten, taught them how to be gentle, how not to pull too hard; the first time I'd done it I had nearly had my finger torn off, and howled in pain. I would stretch my little finger toward them and they would come over, study it for a moment, then start sucking. Their little tongues, warm and viscous like rubber, would wrap around my finger and move against it, creating tiny pockets of air. They would leave when they realized that there was no milk to be had, that no food would come out no matter how long they suckled. Yet the next day they would always come back, as if they had no memory, as if they weren't capable of processing that experience. But really, I think they developed a taste for it eventually; I think they enjoyed it, too.

The boils seemed not to touch the goats, nor the cattle or

any of the other animals. I was sure it had to happen sooner or later. But instead they just faded off me, leaving behind red marks that signaled the places where they had been, reminding me not to expose them or those parts of me that were growing and changing, reminding me to listen to my grandmother.

BOYS

EVERYTHING THAT USED TO BE STORED IN THE ATTIC
had either been moved to the basement or thrown away. The
basement was a cold place at the bottom of the stairs, roughly
the size of our dining room, where I would set foot only when
my mother or my grandmother forced me to—something they
did frequently, with the excuse of sending me to fetch things,
so that I would get used to it (though I never did). All of my
grandfather's clothes that my grandmother hadn't wanted to

throw away were down there, inside an ancient wooden wardrobe that was nearly as old as the house itself. One Sunday my mother decided to take it outside for an airing and to give it a fresh coat of paint. "It's molding," she said. "Who knows how long that's been going on for. Look, see? It's everywhere."

I had never seen my mother take this much interest in anything inside the house. What was even more unusual was that she had taken the initiative herself, choosing to embark on the task without my grandmother having had to ask her again and again to do so. That was what they argued about most often, and I knew how committed my mother usually was to this particular habit of hers.

"How do you plan to get it out of there?" my grandmother asked.

"First I'll empty it," she said. "Then I'll take it up the stairs."

"Don't even think about it," said Grandma. "It's too heavy. You'll break it."

My mother said that she would be careful, her voice taking on that tart, sharp, mouselike tone it took whenever she became irritated.

My grandmother laughed, which only made my mother angrier. So Grandma did what she always did and changed tack. "You'll break your back," she said.

My mother smiled. "I'll get someone to help."

That someone turned up the next day. He was the father of a boy I always used to see in church, and back in primary school, too. The father would pick his son up sometimes when the mother couldn't; I had never seen the two parents together. The boy was called Luca, and he was three years younger than

me. He had started school when I was in third grade. I learned
his father's name only that day; my mother introduced him to
us, to me and Grandma, when he came in through the garden
with another man we later found out was his brother and told
us they were going to help us out with the "men's work." His
name was Stefano. He would turn up at our house again. My
grandma was cold with him that day; she'd understood immediately. She greeted him and told him thanks for "coming all
the way here." That was what she thanked him for, not for his
help—as if she were establishing some kind of distance, drawing a boundary. Then she said she had work to do, and walked
off toward the stables.

"How old are you?" Stefano asked me. He had curly hair
and a soft, somewhat feminine voice.

I told him my age. "You look older," he said. "You must be
in middle school, then."

"She'll be starting her third year soon," my mother replied.

"I should introduce you to Luca," he said, addressing me.
"He'll be starting middle school this year. He's terrified."

My mother laughed. "Of such a small thing! He must take
after you."

She gave him a few seconds to react, holding his gaze with
a half-smile—she had a way of lifting only one side of her
mouth, causing a small dimple to form on her left cheek—
before saying, "Shall we go? The wardrobe is downstairs."

He followed her. I could tell from the way he looked at
her that he was ready to do anything she asked of him. She
didn't even seem to notice. Years later, when it came to be
my turn to move through the world and to decide what form

that movement should take, when it was my time to deal with boys—to really deal with them, to do so deliberately, in ways that were calculated and strategic—I would think back to that day. But in that moment, all I knew was that some part of me stung with jealousy over that manner she had, always so light and seductive, and seemingly unconscious of the fact that all her actions were geared toward ensuring that everyone did her bidding—though as it turned out, and as I would eventually discover, it was in fact the fruit of long sessions in front of the mirror and many nights spent with only herself for company, so that what appeared to be an innate skill had in fact been painstakingly honed over the course of many years into the form she wanted it to take, the form she had envisioned from the very first moment she had set out to work on it.

As I grew older, I learned to discern every trick and every mechanism behind something that appeared to be entirely instinctive. That was what was so exceptional about her: not so much her ability to always get her way, nor that constant seesawing between whimsy and firmness, but how she managed to make invisible all the scaffolding, all the rehearsal that lay behind it.

The wardrobe was brought outside. Stefano and his brother each grabbed an edge and carried it up the stairs, holding it sideways, like a coffin. They set it down on the gravel in the yard and left it open so that the sun would dry it out. My mother offered them some iced tea she'd brewed the night before, along with cookies. Grandma stayed in the stables; her excuse was that the animals needed foddering, and that she had to tend to the vegetable garden. She showed her face just once, for a cursory greeting when they first arrived, and reemerged only after they'd left. She didn't say a word, simply looked at the wardrobe before going back inside the house.

That evening my mother decided that we should eat out. When my father was still around, we would go to a restaurant occasionally. Grandma never came unless there was some reason for it—my birthday or some other grandchild's birthday to celebrate, a christening, a First Communion. So sometimes we would go without her, and the absence of any particular occasion to mark made everything even better. Without Grandma, and away from the immediate surroundings of the house, we could be a family like any other. Mostly it happened in spring or summer, and on the drive out I would get to wind the car window down a little or even all the way without anyone scolding me for it. We would set off before the sun had set, and if it was springtime I would stare at the green meadows and their pink and white flowers lanced by the copper light that filtered over the hills. Sitting in the back of the car, with my mother and father in the front, I would stick my face out and sniff at the new and fragrant air, and those drives would always seem incredibly long to me, as if we were going a little bit farther with every outing.

We would have a pizza in town, or if the weather was good we would go to a hillside restaurant and sit at an outdoor table. My mother would order a bottle of white wine, and they would clink their glasses and take little sips while we waited for our food to arrive. My father would talk and smile, drinking sparingly, while my mother nodded and kept her eyes half-closed when the light shone on her face; she would pick up her glass and slowly drain her wine, savoring its taste, then fill her glass again and smile once more. I would listen only intermittently to their conversation, taking a sip of my Coca-Cola every time I saw my mother pick up her glass, and looking around at the tables beside ours, at the street, at the fading light and the lampposts beginning to switch on.

That night, my mother decided we should go out for pizza. She pulled the car out and waited for me in the driveway with the engine running. I put on the dress Grandma had made for me. She had finished it two days ago: smooth, fine cotton, blue with floral motifs. It reached down to my knees and had puffed sleeves. I thought I might roll them up.

"It suits you," said my mother. "It really suits you. Shall I do your hair up?"

"No, I'll do it."

I pulled the sun visor down as she began to drive.

"I'm hungry," she said. "What will you have?"

"No idea. You?"

"I feel like a ham-and-mushroom pizza today. I don't know why."

She had put on her dark lip liner. I hated when she did that: it made her look like one of those aberrant mothers you saw on films on daytime TV, the kind that lived in mobile homes. Or like C.J. from *Baywatch*. Maybe I would do the same when I got older. I would use a makeup pencil to widen the perimeter of my lips. But I would only do it before I had children.

I could smell her perfume when I sniffed the air coming through the car window. It was as if everything around us—the hills, the fields, the vineyards—smelled of her. The light was dwindling and soon there would be no need for sunglasses; we both kept them on, and everything seemed warmer, the colors richer, as if it were autumn already.

At the pizza restaurant, we looked for a table outside. "For three, please," my mother told the waiter.

"There's only two of us," I said, correcting her.

"No, three," she confirmed. "Stefano is coming, too," she added as the waiter showed us to our table.

We sat down and began to wait. I had lost my appetite and didn't want to be there anymore. I watched the pizzas passing us by on their way to other tables, looking like formless blurs, like brains, like oozing bowels. By the time he arrived, we had already ordered our drinks. I had drunk half of my Coca-Cola, and my stomach was burning. My mother had drunk two glasses of wine, and every now and then her eyes lost focus and she stared into space.

"Sorry I'm late," said Stefano.

His forehead was a little sweaty, his eyes watery. He seemed uglier than when I had seen him that afternoon. He sat down, breathing heavily. "Sorry," he said once more. "I had to go to Luca first. He needed a notebook he had forgotten at my place."

"Don't worry," said my mother. She smiled and took his hand. She kept her eyes fixed on him as if to soothe him, the way you would do with a frightened puppy. I had never seen her be so accommodating with a man. I had never seen her be so accommodating at all. I felt uncomfortable.

"Why don't you bring him round, one of these days? You could spend an afternoon, see the animals."

"Luca is crazy about animals."

"So bring him. That is, if the rumors haven't scared you off."

"What rumors?"

"You don't know?" said my mother. "It's the town's favorite story. We're witches."

I had never heard this story before. Stefano laughed. "What?"

"They say men don't last very long with us. They either leave before too long or they die."

"That's so stupid," said Stefano. "I never listen to the town gossip."

"But it's true. We eat them up."

Stefano laughed again.

"We roast them in the oven, with Christmas stuffing. Or we stew them," she said, laughing her laugh. "You don't believe me. You will."

I watched them laughing and gazing at each other as if they were sitting right across from each other, and much closer than they actually were. I thought they must want to touch each other but were holding back because of me, or perhaps their legs were already touching under the table. I thought of my father in Russia. If the story was real, that would explain why he'd gone: to save himself. Then I told myself I was an idiot for always believing in stories. I told myself I needed to stop being such a child.

•

I LOOKED OUT the car window, the countryside steeped in nighttime, the lights from the houses brushing the edge of the road; I waited until we had gone past the town and reached the fork in the road before I asked her.

"What would you have called me if I'd been a boy?"

She cocked her head to one side, like dogs do. "I've never thought about it."

"Did you always know that I was going to be a girl?"

"No," she said. "I found out when I saw you. But some part of me could feel it. It's what we're destined for, isn't it?"

"Why?"

"Because we're women. And we generate more women. Men don't last with us. That's what everyone says, isn't it?"

"And you believe it?"

"Of course not. People are stupid. Especially people in town."

"Well?" I resumed. "What if I'd been a boy?"

She burst briefly into the lilting, fluttering laugh everyone loved so much, so like the sound of a xylophone. Then she turned serious again.

"I don't know how I would have managed, with a boy. I would have been too jealous. I would never have accepted the thought that he might love someone else more than he loved me. I would have been the world's worst mother-in-law. But I would never have become one. No, I would never have allowed it."

"But what if I had been a boy? What if I'd just been born that way? What would you have done? Would you have abandoned me?"

"What nonsense," she said. "Abandoned. Of course not. But you're not a boy, are you? It's what we're destined for," she repeated.

SEVEN

MY FATHER RETURNED FROM RUSSIA DURING THE
first week of September. He called me one afternoon and
asked if he could come by to see me. He said he would take
me to the city, to the carnival, like he did every year. That
summer's events had made me forget about the carnival, had
made it possible for me not to even think about it. But now, all
of a sudden, it felt like the thing I wanted most in the world,
the thing I had been waiting for all year and with such intense

anticipation that I could think of nothing else, until all that had happened up to that moment seemed irrelevant, minuscule, perhaps even a figment of my imagination, and ceased to worry me.

He came to pick me up from home one morning before lunch. My mother was at work, and Grandma was in the stables. He stopped the car in the driveway and waited there by the porch. I ran toward him, and when he saw me, he opened the car door and stepped out. We embraced, and then he picked me up with a sigh and told me I'd grown. "Are you ready?" he asked. "Shall we go?" I told him I would let Grandma know, and he nodded.

I ran to the stables. I stood at the threshold and called out to tell her that Dad had arrived. "That's fine, go ahead," she said, shouting back. I couldn't figure out where she was. I waited to see if she would emerge, but she stayed where she was. I could hear her working with the pitchfork, moving hay from one place to another. "Bye, Grandma!" I yelled. I waited until she replied, then went back to him.

In the car, my father hugged me again and told me he'd missed me. "I have so many things to show you," he said. He reached for the dashboard and picked up a wooden doll painted in bright colors. "It's a matryoshka," he said. "Remember when I told you about these?"

I studied it for a few moments, and realized I did remember. I opened it up: hidden inside was an identical doll, only smaller. I opened that one up too, then another, and another. It was the first time I'd ever actually held a matryoshka doll. I noticed that the deeper you went and the smaller the doll got, the fuzzier, the more indistinct the details became—from its facial features to the flowers decorating its dress. I put them back, one inside another. "Thank you," I said, and hugged him again. He smelled different.

He put his hands on my waist. "Here you are," he said. He kept his back straight and still, moving his hands up and down my sides until I pulled away. He started the car.

"You have to come and visit me. Before it gets too cold."

"Is it cold already?" I asked.

"It is a little, yes. But everything is so beautiful. The light in the late afternoon. All that open space. You would really like it."

Later, he showed me some photos of his house, said he'd taken them especially for me. I pictured him there, sleeping the way I remembered him sleeping, curled up on his side, and eating meals without us. At the carnival, he took me to the candy stall and let me get almond brittle. It was our ritual, our secret. If even the distance hadn't changed him, then perhaps nothing could.

We sat on a bench. My father chided me for making a mess; the almond brittle had disintegrated and ended up on my pants.

"Look at you, crumbs all over. Just like when you were little," he said, laughing as he cleaned me up. "It still feels like yesterday, you know. When you were little. When you couldn't even walk yet."

A group of older kids came past, shouting as they went. They distracted us for a moment. I watched them as they walked away, then turned back around to look at him.

"What was it like when I was born?" I asked. "Neither of you have ever told me anything about it. Did you see me? Were you with Mom?"

"No. Your grandma was there. But I got to hold you straightaway, afterward. You were warm, and you smelled wonderful. They'd put you in a cream-colored onesie. You had the softest skin I had ever touched."

"Did you ever try to picture what I would be like?"

"Every night. I was happy. We were young, your mother and I, and not prepared for this thing, not prepared for you. We weren't prepared for anything, really, but then you arrived. I saw you, I held you in my arms, and you seemed so little that I thought I might break you—I was afraid I would. That's when I realized that I had to look after you, protect you— and that's a scary thought, you know? But you were there, and you were real—I could touch you and hold you in my arms, and you slept so well, your little face all wrinkly, like someone who's worked very hard and just needs a rest. You slept well when I held you in my arms, and for the first time ever I thought it could be easy after all, that maybe we would actually manage."

He stroked my head. His hands small and warm. "And we did manage. We did a good job."

The light was fading. I looked into his eyes, searching for his pupils, but they were the same color as his irises, and I couldn't find them.

"How's it going with your mother?" he asked.

"Normal."

"Are you good to her? Is she good to you?"

I nodded.

"And your grandma?"

"More and more silent. She never smiles. She's always praying. It must be because of what's been happening."

"What's that?"

"The frogs, the insects, the animals."

"Does she still think it's divine retribution?" He laughed.

I nodded. I could feel my eyes widening, and tried to control them.

"It's what they think in town, too. Everyone does."

"We've never cared what they think in town."

"But what if they're right?"

He took my hand. "It's just superstition," he said. "You mustn't always rely on what your grandma tells you. You mustn't always believe what your mother tells you. They're not liars; it's just that sometimes, they make mistakes. We all do, even if we try not to. You'll understand when you're older. We do try. Listen to me: you must do what you can to keep your mind open. Your mind and your eyes open. And don't pay too much heed to your mother and your grandmother. They might exaggerate sometimes. But they do want what's best for you. You've been a blessing for that place. Keep letting fresh air in; do it for them."

"Is that why you left?" I asked. The words came out unbidden, without my even realizing it. "Were you tired of being with us? Was it too stifling?"

He said no. "Is that really what you think?" he asked.

"You got tired of me. You got tired of us."

I started crying. I tried to hide it: I was embarrassed.

He took me in his arms, squeezing my shoulders and swaying gently back and forth on the bench, as if he were rocking me to sleep.

"Don't think that. I would never have wanted to. You are everything to me, your mother was everything, all of it was everything."

I didn't believe him, but I stayed in his embrace without making a sound, trying to hoard that moment away.

•

"WHAT DID HE say to you?"

She had just taken off her jacket and put her slippers on. She was wearing a black dress that was quite short, and had black stockings on. The outfit was supposed to be dressy, maybe even seductive, but when paired with the slippers, it gave her an oddly comical appearance. My mother had gotten back early that day.

"So?" she asked again, walking up to me. "What did your father say to you?"

Grandma was in the kitchen; my mother knew that, and kept her voice low.

I shrugged. "We went to the carnival."

"That's it?"

"He gave me this."

I took the matryoshka doll out of the front pocket of my backpack, where I had put it that afternoon before going on the rides, nestling it between my pencil-case and a pack of tissues so that it wouldn't get damaged. I showed it to my mom, who picked it up and turned it over in her hands.

"It's so kitsch," she remarked.

"What does that mean?"

"That it's in poor taste," she said, handing it back to me. I looked at it, and it didn't seem in poor taste to me—just different from a few hours ago. The colors seemed more faded. But maybe it was the light at home.

"So what else did he do all afternoon, apart from taking you to the carnival and giving you an ugly wooden doll?"

"It's not ugly," I protested. Then I shrugged again. "He told me about Russia. He showed me some photographs. Of Moscow, of the house where he lives."

"What's it like?"

"Normal," I said. "Small, just one bedroom and the kitchen. But the kitchen is bigger than ours—there's a table and a sofa in the same room. It's got wooden furniture, and . . ."

"Like here," she said. She kept peering into my eyes from up close, as if she could read what was inside me. Then she asked, "Does he live with anyone?"

I didn't say anything . She was still leaning against the wall but with her neck craned toward me, her eyes narrowed, waiting for a response. I shook my head quickly, my throat burning.

"Are you sure?" she asked.

I kept my eyes lowered. I couldn't do anything else.

My mother came up to me, took hold of my shoulders,

and pulled me toward her. I didn't want her to, but I couldn't avoid it.

"I'm sorry," she said, holding me tight against her stomach. "Sorry, sorry, sorry," she repeated as she stroked my hair mechanically, and I pressed my cheek against her dress, inhaling its scent, inhaling the scent of her body, and of what lay beneath.

•

THE HAIL ARRIVED while we were having dinner. The days were still long and hot—not as hot as in the previous months, but enough that we could still eat outside on the porch. But that evening the light faded earlier than usual, and the sky began to darken. It reminded me of my father's encyclopedia with its color charts on the cover: smoke gray, lead gray, anthracite gray. It changed from one moment to the next.

"It looks green over there," said Grandma, as a rumbling began in the distance. "That is not a good sign."

She picked up the napkin from her lap to wipe her mouth, then put it down on the table. "I'm going to gather the animals," she said, before turning to my mother to add, "You should come and give me a hand. We don't have much time."

My mother took one last bite of her food and stood up. The sky lit up for an instant, and shortly after we heard a booming roar that made us all shiver.

"It's getting closer," said Grandma.

I looked at them. "Shall I come, too?" I asked.

"No," said Grandma. "Better not to. You take these things inside."

They headed for the stables, their dresses billowing on improbable gusts of wind that thrashed the grass and the trees and lifted sand from the fields and dust from the road into an ocher cloud—warm and hazy like my mother's photographs from when she was little—that made everything look older and farther away than it was.

I cleared the table. The paper napkins were about to take flight; I managed to catch mine before it was swept away, but my mom's and my grandma's escaped my grasp and began to chase each other across the porch at high speed, as if they were birds, before vanishing in the direction of the fields behind the house. I moved the cutlery, the bottles, and the plates, still laden with food, onto the table in the living room. I gathered the tablecloth with some difficulty, spread it back out on the empty half of the table inside, then set the dishes once more, all of which took me ages. Outside the wind whistled and the shutters on the windows upstairs kept banging, even though they were hooked to the walls. It occurred to me that they should probably be closed, but I decided to wait for my mother and grandmother to come back, because I wouldn't be able to do it on my own. I closed the French doors and sat down again. Through the window I could see leaves whirling, racing from one end of the yard to the other while the sky turned increasingly dark. I wondered if my mother and my grandmother would ever return. I fingered the omelettes they had both left on their plates; they felt cold and rubbery, like a sponge, like something dead.

They came back and knocked on the French doors. It had begun to hail. The wind had mussed their hair and their clothes. They looked like two figures someone had drawn in pencil, then changed their mind and tried to erase, using a finger to furiously rub them off but managing only to blur their features. I opened the doors and they stepped inside, letting in the cold which seemed to have come straight from winter, and the astounding noise of the hail. It sounded like someone was throwing rocks. My mother let out a heavy sigh. "Just in time. That was close."

Grandma said nothing. Their arms were red; they had held them over their heads for protection, and now they were dotted with red marks where the hailstones had hit them.

"Oh dear!" exclaimed my mother, having only just noticed this herself. "We look like we've been stoned," she said, then laughed, looking at my grandmother.

Grandma's hair was wet, half stuck to her head and half in disarray. It looked thinner than normal, as if she had lost some on the way, as if the wind had swept it off. I had never seen her in such a state, and she seemed to realize it, too. "I'm going to dry myself off," she said. "You should do so, too," she added, addressing my mother.

But my mother stayed with me; she hugged me so that I would get wet too, wrung the water out of her hair—which by now reached all the way down to her breasts—then lowered her head, buried her fingers in her locks, and shook them hard. When she lifted her head back up, her hair was curly again, messy and puffed out. "I look like a dog, don't I?" she said, laughing.

She turned toward the window. The hailstones had grown to the size of walnuts.

"What a sight," she said. "It's like the sky breaking into a million pieces."

She put her arms around my shoulders and pulled me closer. We stood watching the scene for a while longer. I could feel her damp dress against my back. We stood in front of the window watching the ice fall on the fields, on the crops, on everything we knew; the green sky, as dark as night, flashing with tendrils of light, creaking over our heads as if all it wanted to do was to fall on top of us.

EIGHT

THE HAILSTORM HAD DAMAGED MY GRANDMA'S VEG-etable garden. The ground was still moist, but already we could see the cracks in the soil; wounds had appeared on the boughs and leaves, and any fruit that was still on the trees—figs, plums, apples—was full of dents. Grandma tasked me with picking all the bruised fruit, which would soon begin to rot.

"If they're damaged, can't we just eat them?" I asked.

"No," she replied. "They have to be discarded."

"Then can't I just leave them there? Won't they fall off anyway?"

"No, you can't," she said. "It's not good to leave them there. A plant will strive to ripen its fruit—all of it. It would be a waste of labor. We have to pick them off so that the plant can put all its energies into generating new fruits and new branches."

I looked around at the trees; some of the fruit was quite high up, and I would need the ladder.

"If anything's a waste of labor, this is it," I remarked.

Grandma stopped in her tracks. "Don't every say that again," she said. "Work is never futile. But not lifting a finger, and always waiting for things to run their course—that is a waste. You know the fate that awaits the idle, those who fail to act."

"No," I said.

"They end up in hell," she said. "Don't let yourself be tempted by what appears to be comfortable. Comfort is for the weak. The devil's there too, sometimes—in weakness."

I watched—her movements quick, her gestures crisp and precise—as she massaged the soil with a curved pitchfork, then used a spade to sift through it, the dark soil rising up like innards or hot soup, until she was satisfied and moved on to another patch. Neve had followed me there, and now she started digging too, as if she were trying to help.

"No," said Grandma. "Make her stop."

I chided Neve a little, but she ignored me.

"I don't know how to," I said. "She never listens to me."

"She doesn't listen to you because she doesn't recognize you. All that excitement when she first arrived, and now you've forgotten all about her."

"That's not true," I protested.

"But it is," she said, crouching low over the earth. "She follows you around, she's always looking for you, but you're never there. Now go get me the ladder."

I obeyed. I called out to Neve and signaled for her to follow me, clapping my palms against my thighs, and eventually it worked. I felt relieved, though not too much. I patted her head, hoping it would count as an apology. I told myself that I really should pay more attention to her.

When we returned with the ladder, I saw Grandma standing still, her head lowered and her hands resting on her belly. But she wasn't massaging it. She was just standing there, motionless, as if she were dead.

"Grandma. Are you all right?"

I ran toward her. I thought she must have begun to feel unwell while she was working. I wasn't sure how much she could endure, at her age.

She nodded, then crossed herself, striking her forehead, her chest, her shoulders with great force, as if she wanted to pierce through, then bringing her closed fist to her mouth and kissing the knuckles, the way she had taught me to do when I was very young and still slept in her room.

"I was just praying," she said. "Why don't you do it, too? You really should. Do you still remember how, or have you forgotten?"

She made me kneel, but she kept standing. "I'm wearing

a dress—it'll get dirty. Your knees are bare and easy to wash. Pray for our home. For the orchard and the fields. Pray for the Lord to forgive your sins. Pray for Him to forgive your mother's too, since she won't pray herself."

I really did pray, as hard as I could, then rapped my fingers against my forehead, chest, and shoulders, just like she had.

·

BACK IN THE HOUSE, my mother was heating up the pasta sauce she and Grandma had made the day before. She had set the table for lunch and readied a pot of water for the pasta, and while she waited for it to boil, she had started making a salad, slicing tomatoes from the vegetable garden, radishes, and carrots.

"Why don't you stop staring and give me a hand," she said. "You look like you've been embalmed."

I went toward her and tried to see what I could do. I always felt out of place, and clumsy too, in that kitchen when both of them were around. "Never mind," my mother huffed. "You know what you can do? Go down to the laundry room. The washing machine will be done by now. Bring the laundry up and hang it outside. Go on, I'm sure you can manage."

The washing machine had indeed run through its cycle. I opened the door and stuck a hand inside: the load was still warm and smelled of turquoise. Next to it stood the tub of washing powder. I lifted the lid; there was the plastic dosing ball. It had been years since I had last picked it up, but it felt exactly as I remembered it: supple and rubbery. Once, when

I was little, Grandma had caught me playing with it. I hadn't been doing much, just filling it up with powder and emptying it out again. The powder was white and smelled good; it looked like sand, so I pretended that it was. I imagined that I was on this perfumed beach, the sea full of foam, gurgling and blowing bubbles. I scooped up the powder, inhaled its scent, and felt safe. Then I poured it out over one end of the tub and added more on top, making a mountain of sand like I would do at the beach. When I was satisfied with the result, I ran my hand over it until everything was back in its place, until the powder in the tub was perfectly level, and raked my fingers through it like plows. Grandma found me hunched over like that, with my head almost all the way inside the tub, and scolded me.

"Get up right now. That is not a toy."

Later on I realized that she must have been afraid that I would swallow some of the powder, or even just put my fingers in my mouth and give myself chemical poisoning. But in that moment I was too young to understand, and so I burst into tears, frightened by her tone and by the feeling that I had been caught doing something I shouldn't have. She took me to wash my hands, to get rid of the washing powder and calm my sobbing, and when my mother heard me crying, she came over to ask Grandma what had happened, and got angry at her. She lifted me up and took me outside, into the fields, to survey our land; she held me all the way, even though I wasn't so little anymore and must have already been quite heavy to carry. She rocked me back and forth, pretending every now and then to drop me, all so that I would crack a smile. It was the only time she ever comforted me like that, taking her time over it, without losing interest or changing her mind until she had gotten what she wanted anyway.

I decided to play with the powder again that day, but I was older now, and no matter how hard I strained my imagination, it didn't feel like the beach anymore. Still, I leaned toward the tub of detergent and inhaled deeply, and found the same scent too in the laundry, damp and fluffed up like an enormous white cloud. I stayed that way for a while, then sat back on my haunches, the floor a cold contrast against my skin, which had been warmed up by the sun and the heat outside. The hair on my arms prickled, and a tremor coursed through my body. I felt the urge to touch myself, so I did, quickly, breathing in the scent of clean laundry and of the washing powder that used to remind me of the beach and in which I would run my fingers until my fingers smelled of it too and I could feel the grains under my fingernails.

I must have had detergent on my fingers because the more I touched myself, the more it burned. But I kept going until I began to shake, my mind clouding, the smell of the laundry and the powder growing thicker, and the burn down there working its way through the pleasure to where I knew it would cleanse me, like fire or salt on a wound, like the stories Grandma told.

•

STEFANO STAYED FOR DINNER that evening. He had offered to help repair the damage from the hailstorm—holes in a couple of shutters, dents in the roof of the shed. It had hailed again in the afternoon, just after lunch, but now the sky looked calm. Nevertheless, my mother set the table inside.

Grandma didn't say a word throughout, only minding what was on her plate. The one time she made her voice heard was when my mother wheeled out the old egg story. She often did this; it was one of those stories about me that she was fond of telling, kept at the ready for whenever the conversation languished. I have never understood why she loved it so much.

"When she was three or four years old, Valentina buried an egg," she began, as usual. "She was convinced that it would sprout a hen."

"It was an experiment," I grumbled. "I was little."

"Do you remember?" she asked my grandma.

Grandma began to laugh. It was one of the few things that always made her laugh.

"A chick," she clarified. "She knew that chicks come before hens. I'd taught her that."

"Well, anyway, Valentina dug a hole in the ground next to the vegetable garden, and put an egg inside. Then she covered it up."

"She used to watch me planting seeds," said Grandma. "She must have thought it worked the same way."

"A chick plant!" my mother laughed. "You should give it another go sometime."

"Maybe I will," I said, shrugging.

Stefano was laughing, too. He caught my eye and smiled at me for a moment, his eyes bright and encouraging, as if he wanted to reassure me.

After that, there was silence again. Grandma said, "Excuse me," as if it were a command, then got up and went upstairs.

It was just the three of us left now. My mother and Stefano were still laughing, looking at each other, brushing each other's hands.

Later, once they had cleared the table (they did this together, without my help; it was the first time I had ever seen a man do household chores), they sat on the porch and smoked cigarettes. I could hear them whispering. Sometimes their voices sounded sharp, and sometimes they were rough and low. Just before I went to bed, I began to listen out for what they were saying.

"I think that's what they're for, mothers. Two things: bringing us into the world and nursing us on guilt. Makers, manufacturers of guilt. That's what I call them. It's how they keep us bound to them."

"For all your life," he said. "There's no way out of it."

"No. There's no way out."

•

BY THE TIME I heard my mother go up to her room, it was very late. The stairs creaked slowly, as if she were pausing for a minute between every step. In my imagination she looked different, her hair tousled and blowing in the wind, sticking to her face, her forehead, her eyes, a sinister grin curling her lips.

I knew what awaited us now, but it was late to arrive. That was enough to lull me into thinking I was saved, that I might have gotten away with it after all. The blood had not returned yet, and maybe it would be the same with all the other stuff, too. I assumed the prayers must have worked, that no matter how many sins I had committed, every time I got down on my knees and spoke to the Lord, asked Him to forgive me, to please, please stop making me grow, stop punishing me this way and leave the house alone, He had actually been listening, and ended up feeling guilty about it all.

•

SCHOOL WAS DUE to start soon; it was September already, and you could feel it in the air. The days ended sooner and sometimes it rained—I would wake up with cold feet and no light reaching my eyes—and Ilaria and I had to stay indoors. We took the opportunity to catch up on our summer homework. It had been that way every year since primary school: the last two weeks of the holiday always flew by because we had too much homework left to do. Even though our parents tried, come June every year, to impress upon us the importance of managing our time properly, of doing a little bit of homework every day and not leaving it all to the last few weeks, with every passing year they had become less vigilant—if presumably for different reasons—about whether we actually did so, and we paid them less and less heed. With everything that had happened that summer, Ilaria and I had barely even opened our schoolbooks. Our reasons differed, and we kept them from each other; but in that moment, when we realized it was only a matter of days before school started again, everything was as it had always been. This was how it worked: Ilaria did the math and geometry assignments, I handled Italian and history, and then we copied off each other. In this way we managed to halve the amount of homework we each had to do. It was a system we'd had in place since third grade, and in spite of everything, we stuck to it in September 1996, too.

We would start in the morning. Usually I went over to Ilaria's; her parents were out and her brother was often at their grandparents', so the house was empty and there was nobody to catch us copying each other's work—though we made sure we changed a few words here and there in the Italian and history homework so that they wouldn't turn out exactly the same. If Ilaria's mother had found us out, she'd have grounded Ilaria and told my mother and grandmother about it. She was always going on about how not doing your homework properly was tantamount to cheating, and how much it would hold us back during the school year. She taught at a high school in the city, and I could just imagine her giving her own students the same lecture, and how boring they must think she was. Her voice was high-pitched and always a little too loud, as if she were trying to make herself heard in every corner of the classroom even when she was only talking to her daughter or to her husband, right next to her.

If it was a sunny day we would use the table on their terrace, and if not we'd sit on the sofa inside. We would turn the television on, glancing at music videos and children's programs in between exercises. We would eat snacks on the sofa—chocolate milk, bread and Nutella, and potato chips, which we had to buy from the bakery downstairs because they never had any at home. Her mother would pick up Ilaria's brother from their grandparents' house and come home at five o'clock. We would take the clock from their parents' bedside table and put it in the living room, setting the alarm for half past four. In that half hour we would eliminate the crumbs from the sofa and stash any empty chip and snack wrappers in my backpack, switch off the TV, and move to the dining table, where we would continue to copy each other's homework from the morning at lightning speed until we heard the front door open.

"Do you think they'll make us do the same old thing again this year? Write about our summer holiday?" I groaned. "They've really got no imagination."

"Well, it shouldn't be too hard for you," said Ilaria.

I looked up from my notebook. She was still copying furiously.

"Why?"

She stopped and lifted her gaze. "You've had a lot going on, this summer."

"What do you mean?"

"I mean over at your place. What's happening at your house," she said, holding her pen at half-mast. It was obvious that she was weighing her words.

"Which is what?" I insisted. "What's happening at my house?"

"Well . . ." she began. "Your father. Then the insects. The animals. Oh, and by the way," she added, "I'm sorry. About the hailstorm and what happened to your vegetable garden."

I said nothing, staring right into her eyes. "Who told you that?"

"Everyone in town is talking about it."

It must have been Marco. I was sure of it. I asked her if it was.

"No," she said. "Why would it be Marco?"

"He came by yesterday. He saw the vegetable garden. He's the only one who could have told you."

"It wasn't him. Why was he at your place yesterday?"

I decided I wasn't going to stop. Or maybe I couldn't stop. I felt as if I had been backed into a corner, and the only thing I could do to break free was to attack. "I didn't want to tell you, but it's the truth; we've been meeting up. Even when you're not around. We're seeing each other."

I don't really know why I did it, why I told her about it. I often wondered about it afterward. There had been no reason to do so. Marco hadn't told her anything—that much was obvious from her reaction. And yet I didn't believe her. In that moment, I couldn't: I doubted him and I doubted her, as if everything I had ever known had been called into question. It left a scar deep inside me. I never really trusted anyone after that.

It hurt her, too. I found it more of a struggle to tell the truth than to tell lies; that much was certain. I kept flinging it at her as if I were throwing rocks at a window for a dare: from a distance, determined to hit the mark, then quickly fleeing the scene. And this was the kind of truth that could shatter glass into a thousand pieces. Later, I would feel guilty all over again for having told her the truth instead of a lie.

Ilaria was angry. We had never had a real argument

before, never really perceived each other that way. We were twelve years old, and nobody, not even our parents, knew us as well as we knew each other. I will never forget her expression, nor the self-awareness I felt in that moment: of being somehow larger than I was, as if she were shrinking and I were growing, of having the power to decide what to do with her—disappoint her, push her away, cause her pain. In that moment, or maybe later on, I realized that this must be what my father had been talking about: the feeling of having control over another person, of cradling them in your hands like the tiniest and most fragile of beings.

"If you must know," she hissed, "everyone's always talking about you. They say you're witches. That everything's that happened to your house, you've brought upon yourselves."

"And you believe that?" I said, laughing.

"I didn't, no. Because you were my friend."

She told me she never wanted to see me again. It didn't really affect me much in the moment. It was just another change, one of the many that had taken place over those last few months, hurled from the heavens and onto my doorstep. When you have been suffocating for so long—just as when you have been in pain—you develop a kind of apathy. You become conditioned.

•

MY MOTHER CAME to pick me up after work. Ilaria's parents hadn't arrived yet. I left her house in silence—in silence, after the words we had screamed at each other and that I could still hear ringing in my ears. The house was empty, and I thought of how I was never going to see her again. I didn't feel any pain, only a little bit of nostalgia.

My mother didn't say anything. She wasn't very good at figuring out when something was wrong—not as good as Grandma, anyway. Or maybe I had learned how to pretend. The wind had picked up. The air was whistling through the windows, so loud that we couldn't hear the radio anymore.

I remember we were still on the street, near the driveway, and I could already tell from there that something wasn't right. The walls of our house, and especially the blind wall, were no longer white. As we got closer, they looked like they were moving. Sickly, covered with dark rashes and dots, as if they'd caught the measles.

Grandma was outside, staring fixedly at a specific spot on the wall. She was sitting on the ground, and I thought she must be feeling unwell.

As soon as the car stopped, I ran to her while my mother turned the engine off.

"Grandma." Her eyes were wide open and dry, as if she could no longer move her eyelids. "Grandma, are you all right?"

"See?" she said. "I was right. See?"

She paused, gasping, and after a deep shuddering breath, she spoke again. She did it all without ever breaking her stare, as if she hadn't even recognized me, as if she would have said what she was about to say to anyone who happened to walk up to her then.

This time even my mother had had enough. She made

me get back in the car and made Grandma get in, too. Then she ran to the house, covering her head to protect it from the swarm of black locusts leaping wildly all around her, and shifting in the air like pollen buffeted by the wind. They were smaller than any I had seen before; they clung to the walls and to the plants as if to lay their claim over them. My mother went inside and quickly came back out, carrying a gym bag. When she got back into the car, the creatures were crawling all over her hair and clothes.

"They're everywhere," she said.

Some leapt from her to me, even though I tried to evade them. Grandma sat quietly in the backseat. Her eyes were lowered and her hands were clasped, like when she would sit on her bed and pray the rosary. But she wasn't praying right now; she just looked tired.

"What will we do?" I asked.

"Well, we're definitely not sleeping here tonight," said my mother. "We'll stay in a hotel."

Grandma looked up. "No," she said. "You go. I'm staying here."

Mom rolled her eyes, a gesture Grandma hated and always rebuked her for. "Don't make this into some kind of tragedy now," my mother replied. "It'll only be for one night. Tomorrow we'll call pest control. Or an exorcist, I guess."

"You think this is funny?" said Grandma. Her voice was low and hoarse. "You think everything is funny. You think everything is a game."

My mother shook her head. She looked like she was about to say something, but instead she started the engine.

"I told you I'm not coming. Drop me off at the door so I can get inside faster."

"I'm not leaving you anywhere. You're coming with us."

"Fine. I'll go by myself," said Grandma. "Cover your face, Valentina," she added, then stepped out of the car and right into that crackling storm.

She was quick to close the car door behind her, but not quick enough. The car filled up with black locusts, and I turned around to watch Grandma going back toward the house with her arms raised to protect her head, shielding herself as best she could. I thought of Neve. I couldn't see her anywhere. I called out her name. "She'll be fine," said my mother. "She'll keep Grandma company. They'll hole up inside the house and they'll be fine. Grandma knows how to handle herself."

We drove back toward town. I kept staring at the house, at its blind white walls covered with dark, wriggling stains, until it disappeared from sight.

•

WE STAYED IN a hotel that night. We went all the way to the city and booked a room. It had three stars and windows that faced out onto the street. "Do you like it?" my mother asked me. She seemed to know the place already. I nodded, though I didn't really care. I had been in a hotel only twice before, many years ago, on holidays with her and Dad. When we went to the seaside with Grandma we rented a flat or a serviced apartment. But it was exciting enough just to be there, in the city, as if we'd been kicked out of our own home. I forgot all about the invasion of the locusts, of Grandma inside that black storm. My mother was smiling again; perhaps she had forgotten, too.

We called down to the reception desk for our dinner, and arranged to have it delivered to our room.

"I bet this'll cost us," said Mom after she'd put the phone down. Then she shrugged. "But I don't mind. We never get to have any fun. It'll be like a holiday. That's what it feels like, no?"

There was a double bed in the room with an orange bedspread that matched the checkered wallpaper. There was a wall-to-wall carpet, which seemed glorious to me back then, and so unusual. A furry floor. I took my shoes off and started pacing back and forth, squeezing my toes into the carpet as if to cling to it. The window faced the street, but we were so high up that the city looked different. It was already dark outside, a warm glow around the lampposts, cars passing by. I liked the city.

Our dinner was brought in by a uniformed waiter pushing a two-tiered trolley like the kind I had only ever seen in the movies. If only the dishes had come with silver covers, it would have been perfect.

"They might have done that if we'd ordered hot food," said my mother. "Or maybe they save those for a certain kind of dish. Dishes for posh people. If we'd ordered spaghetti with lobster sauce, perhaps. Or duck à l'orange."

She laughed, then bit into her sandwich. "We'll do it next time," she said, talking with her mouth full. "Next time we'll dress up real nice and pretend we're countesses. We'll order stuffed guinea fowl and we'll eat it right here in bed. That's the kind of thing rich people do. I'd quite like a row of pearls around my neck and feathers in my hair. Why not?"

We finished our sandwiches and drank our Coca-Colas. It was all a bit strange, but I quickly realized how easy it would be to get used to it. Very soon it felt as if we had always behaved this way—as if we'd made a habit of eating in bed and all the rest of it. Even the room began to look familiar; it was as if home and Grandma no longer existed.

We lay down next to each other, my mother's arm wrapped around me and holding me close while the television screen right in front of us showed the evening programs.

"Here we are," she said. "Just like when you were little. You know, when you were born, I didn't want to look at you. I was young, Vale, I was very young. It would be like you having a baby six years from now—can you imagine? And nine months is a long time, long enough to change your mind many times over. But then I saw you, I held you in my arms. You were all red and bloodied, all shriveled up, a little scary-looking. But you were mine, you had come out of me. You were there, and you were real. It's a strange thing to have a child—you'll understand one day. It's something that you've created but that you cannot, *must* not destroy, otherwise you're damned for all eternity. It's a thing that relies on you, that you must protect, make sure nothing bad ever happens to it. But bad things happen regardless, and by the time you've noticed, there's nothing you can do about it."

Only then did I remember the locusts again, and I thought that it must be true, that they really must have come from me—and I felt strong, and I felt powerful.

NINE

IT WAS THE LIGHT COMING THROUGH THE WINDOW that woke us up. We'd forgotten to draw the curtains, and up there on the sixth floor, the sun shone in unfiltered. At home we were used to having trees around, thick foliage screening the light, and our little windows covered by the shutters my grandma closed every evening before going to sleep. Total darkness at night, light in the morning: that was how the house breathed, she said; that was how we would breathe better.

I think we must have thought of Grandma at the same time, as soon as we woke up. We didn't say anything, neither then nor later on, but I know she was the first thing both of us thought of. Grandma, the house, what we had left behind. The black locusts, which would surely find their way inside, if they hadn't already. The hotel room looked different in the daylight; the orange wallpaper seemed older, stale, imbued with the breath of the countless guests who must have stayed there over the years. We got dressed without speaking. My mother was smiling still, forcing herself to do so, but I already knew even then that nothing was as it had been the night before.

We went back down to the ground floor, my mother settled the bill, and we set off. It was still early, and not a working day. I remember the clear road, the slow cars in the faint light as we overtook them. Once we made it out of the city, the air changed. It was fresh and delicate, fragrant with the aroma of dried leaves and suffused with the muddy scent of wet, mown grass. There was also the smell of the encroaching autumn, which I hadn't been able to detect in the city; those few hours without it had felt like a liberation. Like breathing in the smell of bleach from the walls.

When we arrived, we walked into the house without saying a word. Neve was inside, as was Luna. They were both desperate to get out. Grandma wasn't there. She wasn't in the house, and she wasn't in the vegetable garden. But the locusts were everywhere. They hopped over the fields and the courtyard. They clung to the walls like black pustules. They were inside the house, too; Grandma must have accidentally left some door or window open. They moved in clusters, holding still for a few seconds or a minute at a time, then leaping into the air all together, varying the parabola of their flight every time. They kept chirping. The whole house the whole hill seethed with the noise they made.

We looked for Grandma, called out her name. I was the one who found her, facedown on the ground in the vineyard. The locusts looked like they were feasting on her body.

·   •

WHEN I WAS LITTLE, about seven years old, I watched a TV documentary about the midnight sun and the polar night.

Light after twilight and darkness during the day.

In Norway, in Iceland, in those enduringly cold countries close to the North Pole where the sky was as white as ice, light and dark took turns with each other for six months at a time. During the summer you could go out in the middle of the night and see where your feet were going, no streetlights needed, and you could run around in the fields and go for walks, the light as thin as the glow from a lampshade, but alive. In winter you woke up and went to sleep in the dark, and that was how it was all the time, for six months. People didn't go out much; they stayed at home like hibernating bears.

Grandma was lucid only at night. In the daytime, as the hours of light grew colder and shorter, she slept, or lay with her eyes half-open and staring at nothing at all, or moaned in discomfort, depending on how much morphine she'd been given and whether it had taken effect yet. One day her usual dose wasn't enough, and she began to rant and rave. Not against anyone in particular—just into empty space.

I had never heard her utter those kinds of words before. She even blasphemed. Twice, in two different ways, her voice tight and rough. Then the nurse walked in. She had been coming every day except for Saturdays and Sundays, which were always the worst. She gave Grandma an injection through her drip, and Grandma gradually calmed down, spluttering like the carburetor in a lawn mower before finally falling asleep.

It was in the evenings that the morphine seemed to have the best effect, leaving her awake but sedated. That was when my mother and I would talk to her.

My mother would go in with a tray and help her eat. She would close the door behind herself, wanting to be left alone in there. I could hear her talking softly behind the wall, and Grandma too, her voice straining, her sentences brief, her answers empty. I don't think her attitude toward my mother, toward us both, changed at all, which was surprising. We would examine what was left of her body, a dry, white shell, the scaly skin of an albino snake, which I refused to touch for fear that it would shrink away, that it would fall off like a molting animal's, that it would crumble into pieces. We would watch it lie inert for hours until it would suddenly wake into restless movement, trying to roll over, to get up, with the slow, clumsy gestures of a reptile; we would watch it curse when it failed, and plead with its eyes, all through the day until it was finally time for the morphine again.

"What's wrong with her?" I asked my mother. "Why is she acting like this?"

"It's her stomach," she replied. "The doctor says it's some-thing in her stomach. He wants to run more tests."

"Is it a tumor?"

"I don't know. They don't know," she replied, shaking her head and clasping one of my shoulders. "Let's not think about it," she said, holding back tears as she hugged me.

Early in the morning my mother and the nurse would open the shutters and air out the room, but sunlight seemed to make Grandma worse. Like a vampire or some kind of demon, she would cringe and moan when she saw the light. At night she was herself again, weaker and wearier perhaps, but her expression and her words were her own again.

Stefano came by every day. He helped the nurse change the bedsheets, and he checked Grandma's pulse when the nurse wasn't there; he volunteered for the Red Cross, so he knew what he was doing. Grandma had learned to endure his presence wordlessly. She even allowed herself to be picked up when she was too weak to stand. She could hardly look at him, but she let him do it anyway.

When my mother was at work in the afternoons, he came instead.

"What do you think?" he asked me once.

"There's nothing to think," I replied.

"How old are you now?"

"Twelve."

He sat with me while I did my homework. He looked at my notebook, where algebraic expressions lay unfinished and erased.

•

IT WAS WHEN the sun stopped rising that I finally managed
to speak to her.

"What should I do, Grandma? Tell me what I need to do
to make everything stop."

"Give my leg a rub, for a start. A good rub, mind you; it's
gone numb."

So I did, but through the blanket, because I couldn't bear
to touch her skin. I rubbed that blanket as hard as I could,
just as she demanded ("Harder, I said. I told you I can't feel
a thing. Harder. You're not scared, are you?"), and without
dwelling too much on how stiff and still her legs felt, or on
how they seemed to shrink with every touch.

I turned away. The shutters on the window were still open.
We had opened them in the morning in the hopes of letting
some light in, but the sun had never showed, and no one had
thought to close them. The whole countryside was submerged
in the same thin, dark fog that usually came in November or
February. But it was still only September.

"The sun didn't rise today, Grandma," I said. "What should
I do?"

"What's it got to do with you?" she said. "It would be no
use at all."

"It's my fault. I'm worried that it's my fault."

Grandma rubbed her stomach and held back a grimace.
"You see?" she said. "It hurts right here. This tumor is like a

baby; it kicks out to remind you it's there. But I'll be damned if I ever forgot, not for a single day in my whole life."

I told her what I'd read. About the sacrifices.

"Maybe I could do something, Grandma. Then maybe God would calm down and stop tormenting us."

"If it is what we deserve, so it shall be."

Then she looked at me, and for the first time in a very, very long time, she smiled at me.

"You take after me," she said. "When I was little, the nuns would put me in detention. I would always run away—I couldn't abide the thought that someone should tell me what to do. I wasn't used to it. My mother had died, my father worked, and I was the eldest of my siblings."

"How did your mom die?" I asked, since no one had ever told me before.

"In childbirth," she replied. "It was common enough, back then. Babies were born dead, or they killed their mothers, or they both died."

"And the baby? Did it die, too?"

"No," she said. "It was your uncle Michele. My father picked him up and lifted him to the sky while my mother lay dying in a pool of her own blood."

Grandma had six siblings. Seven children if you counted her. Michele was the only boy. I could just picture her poor mother, my great-grandmother (in my head, she always looked old) giving birth six times, always to girls. Six girls who could have been twins; I could see that from the photographs my grandma kept on her chest of drawers, how they had looked even more alike when they were younger. My great-grandmother had yearned for a baby boy, if only to appease my great-grandfather—Grandma told us that he had threatened to find another woman if his wife didn't deliver a boy—only to die just as the boy finally arrived, without even being granted the blessing of looking at him.

"That was when I made my request," said Grandma.

She was smiling again. It was strained, barely a trace of it there, but it was a smile. It wasn't for me, not like before. Instead, she seemed to be smiling to herself.

"What do you mean, Grandma?"

"I asked to never have boys."

"Who did you ask?"

"The Lord."

I looked at her and I pictured the scene—I'm not sure if it was right then and there or maybe a little later, but either way, that's what I did. I pictured her yelling and cursing and screaming at God. Railing at Him, and at her father, and at the newborn: traitorous men, men who had betrayed the woman who had loved and nurtured them, who would have served them for years to come. That is how I pictured her, not just asking, but demanding to never, ever give birth to boys, only girls—for if her mother hadn't caved, if she hadn't prayed day and night to the Lord for a baby boy, if she hadn't surrendered to the foolish expectations of some oafish man, she would still be alive. I pictured her blaspheming against God, that God who had allowed such a thing to happen, and a moment later—like a stubborn child—invoking Him to heed her prayers, to direct all of His loathing onto her father. I imagined her forgiving

Him, forgiving the God her mother had loved so much, so long as He joined forces with her, so long as He took her side against her father, the man she would never be able to absolve.

And He had listened. He had given her only girls, and the same to her daughters, too.

"I asked the Lord, and He listened. But maybe the devil was listening, too. Or maybe this is what it was always going to cost," she said. "The price to pay."

She closed her eyes and sighed. She looked like she wished she were gone. I thought I should ask her one more time, before it was too late.

"I could get some doves, like it says in the book. Or one of the goats. I could do it, if it'll stop Him."

"That's not done anymore," said Grandma. "We don't do sacrifices anymore. How many times have I told you already? What you have to do is confess, and pray. Go to Father Gianni, confess your sins, then pray for us all."

But I didn't. What happened instead is that I waited for Grandma to fall asleep, and for my mother to fall asleep too, before creeping downstairs and going to the goat pen. I picked one out and took it with me, far away from all the others, far from the house, to a place where no one would hear us.

It was the darkest night I had ever witnessed. There must have been thick clouds covering the stars and the moon, and even the lampposts and the lights from other people's homes. I pointed a flashlight at the grass in front of my feet to find my way, dragging the goat I'd chosen behind me. I had put Neve's leash on it. I took it to the vegetable garden and went behind the cowshed so that even if my grandma or my mother were to look out the window, they would not be able to see me. I dug a hole in the ground with one hand and held on to the leash with the other, then planted the flashlight in the hole. The shaft of light struck the goat's snout, and the goat started bleating.

Calm down now.

I moved it out of the light and began to stroke its back. It was only a few weeks old, and I hadn't gotten to know it yet. There had been so much going on that I no longer even noticed what was happening with the animals. Not the nice things, at any rate. I noticed only when something terrible happened, something I could blame myself for. I think that by then, that feeling—that guilt—had turned into a kind of drug. I couldn't even remember where it had all started; all I knew was that it was the way things were, the way things were meant to be, and the knowledge that it was all on me, that everything depended on me, made me feel better.

One time, after the failed experiment with the egg, I had managed to grow a plant from a carrot I had put in the ground. I was seven years old, and Grandma's vegetable garden was big and flourishing. In the summer we got cherries, peaches, plums, and apricots; in winter we had apples, pears, citrus fruits, and vegetables, too: lettuce, tomatoes, zucchinis, pumpkins, cauliflower. We also had some other things I don't remember because we didn't really eat them (beetroot, perhaps?), things that Grandma rarely kept for us but that did well in the market. Grandma was capable of growing anything she wanted, and I aspired to be just as good as her. I pulled out a carrot. Grandma had taught me how: you had to use both hands to grasp the leaves that sprouted from the soil, plant your feet properly with your legs spread wide, and pull as hard as you could. If you failed to distribute your strength in the right manner, the leaves would tear and the carrot would remain buried in the soil, so you had to make sure you were concentrating. I carefully extracted the carrot, then planted it in the spot where I played my games, under the old horse chestnut tree near the ditch that filled up with green, soupy, stagnant water every time it rained. I planted my carrot—only the head, cutting off the rest and feeding it to the chickens—and I waited: for days, for weeks. Every day I would go over to check on it until finally I got my reward. More carrots. The seed had spread. They continued to proliferate and grow for a while—at least that's what it looked like from the leaves, which got taller and taller—and then they died. I don't know why. I guess I didn't tend to them as was required, and I lacked the knowledge needed for their proper cultivation—the kind of knowledge my grandmother had never passed on to my mother, and that she wasn't passing on to me, either. Or maybe I was the one who refused to be taught, who never asked, or asked but didn't listen, or forgot a moment later. The world was moving in a different direction; even I could tell, though I was still little.

I took the goat to my spot, the place where I had planted the carrot in what must have felt, in that moment, like an infinitely long time ago. The ditch was still there, though there were only leaves, rocks, and dry grass in it now. Grandma didn't slaughter livestock anymore, not since Grandpa had died, but she used to before, and this was the place where she did it. I had been unaware of this fact at the time of the carrots; I was told only later on. This was where she and Grandpa would bring the beasts, at least the larger ones: calves, kids, pigs (they kept pigs too, at the time). They would bring them here so that their blood would drain into the ditch instead of seeping into the soil, instead of flooding it. The ditch was full of water back then and ran farther, flowing past the house and pouring into some stream below. My mother said it would turn red every time they took the animals to slaughter. Red rivers flowing around the house. My mother and her sisters were used to it; they'd grown up with it. They didn't think there was anything grisly or gruesome about it. All it meant was that it must be nearly Christmas or Easter, or that summer was almost over.

The goat had stopped bleating. It trusted me. I kept stroking its head and back. It trusted me. When I stopped and let go of its leash, it looked around and made no attempt to move. It bowed its head, sniffed at the grass, and began to graze. It continued to trust me when I put my hand in my pocket and brought out the knife I'd taken from the kitchen, and it still trusted me when I placed the blade against its neck. It did not even lift its head; it had no reason to do so.

DARKNESS

EVERYTHING WAS DIFFERENT IN WINTER. THE TREES lost their leaves and their ability to isolate us from the rest of the world. You'd wake up one morning and suddenly you could see the other houses on the hill, the fields, the road, the footpaths and the people who walked along them on week- ends when the weather was good. Then the fog would come, either the thin kind, like a wet, gray cobweb that blurred the outline of things and put you to sleep, or white and thick, so heavy that if you stood at the window you couldn't see the stables, and if you lay on the grass—as I did in the morning sometimes when I didn't have to go to school, lying there until the chill of the frost filtered through my clothes—you could hardly make out your own toes. When the first snow arrived, and if there was enough of it, I would stay at home and skip school, as it was impossible to drive until the snowplow had been through, and it would have taken far too long to walk.

I never remembered, during the summer, how long those days could be.

But once again they arrived, starting around the middle of October, not a day earlier or later than they would have been expected to. They arrived at the right moment, as they always had for as long as I could remember, for as long as my mother and my grandmother before her could remember. They arrived as they always did, convincing us that everything was in the past now. That summer and all that it had brought would soon be nothing but a memory.

Grandma was feeling better. She could get out of bed again. She wasn't back to the way she had been before, she couldn't work all day as she used to, but she could still feed the beasts and harvest the vegetables. It took her more effort to bend over, her mouth tight and her brow furrowed, but she insisted on doing it herself. The doctor who came to check on her twice a week would shake his head as he left. "She shouldn't be working like this. She shouldn't even be out of bed."

"You thought she was never getting up at all," my mother pointed out. "She wasn't supposed to make it to the end of the week."

"I can't explain it," said the doctor. "But it's certainly for the best."

"She knows what's best for her," my mother replied, and that was the end of that debate.

She did the cooking now, but only because Grandma permitted it. Grandma ate with us at the dinner table, not in bed. "This isn't a hospital. Only dogs and prisoners eat where they sleep. And people in the hospital," she'd say, complaining every time that there wasn't enough salt or there was too much of it, that something had been cooked wrong, that some key ingredient was missing.

"Just like in the hospital, see?" she'd whisper to me. "Your mother wants me to feel like I'm in the hospital. I wouldn't touch this pasta even if I were missing all my teeth," she'd say, with a half-smile and a wink at me, before lifting her gaze again and assuming a more somber expression.

My mother was sitting far enough away not to hear—or she pretended not to. She had changed, after what had happened to Grandma. She had changed more than even Grandma had. She no longer talked back to Grandma; she was like a different person. She was like one of my aunts; they always worried about Grandma and bore her cutting remarks with their eyes lowered. It must have been because of the fright she'd had when she had almost lost Grandma forever. But I had the impression that there was something else to it, too. The feeling scared me, sometimes. It felt like I hardly knew who they were anymore.

My father had called to ask how Grandma was doing. First he'd spoken to my mother, who'd muttered into the phone for a few minutes through gritted teeth before passing it to me.

"The line's not very good here," he'd said. "But this young lady sounds like she's grown up since I last saw her! How tall are you now?"

I thought I was probably as tall as I had been before, but I had put on weight on my chest and my belly. I checked the gap between my thighs every night, hoping it was still there. "As long as there's space between your legs, you count as skinny," Ilaria used to say. "That's what my grandma told me." My thighs did touch if I squeezed them, but if I held my breath I could fit two, even three fingers in between. There was hair growing on my crotch now, and in my armpits too, where it was getting harder to hide. I shaved it off every now and then, using the razor my father had left behind. It made me think of him every time.

"Well?" he said. "How tall are you?"

"As tall as before," I said. "Maybe an extra centimeter."

"A whole centimeter!" he said, laughing. "I might not recognize you anymore if I saw you on the street."

The connection was poor. His voice was grainy, overlaid by whistling, rasping noises that made it sound like he was standing in the middle of a tropical rainstorm or a meteor shower. That was how I pictured him, inside a phone booth in a lunar landscape, surrounded by darkness and by white and gray boulders, trying to shield his head and evade the falling stars. I realized that I couldn't really remember his features, that no matter how hard I tried, his face remained indistinct and out of focus, as if I were looking at him through a pane of grimy glass. I hoped he would speak again; maybe with a little effort I might be able to reconstruct his face through his voice. But all I heard was a rustling, and after that the line got cut off.

•

I WOULD HAVE liked to tell him that things had become harder since he'd left. I would have told him, but he did not call back. He would have taken me with him if he had known that Grandma had become stricter now, that she prayed even more than before and forced me to do it too. She would check my knees every evening; if they were chafed, it meant that I had been praying. I would kneel beside the bed with my hands clasped over the mattress, as if I were really doing it. But instead I would squeeze my legs together and think of Marco, or of Stefano stroking the back of my mother's neck and her arms, and brushing against her breasts, and staring at me sometimes when I set the table or leaned over to feed the chickens. My father would have taken me with him if he had known that my mother had been slinking out of bed like a mischievous child, tiptoeing down the stairs, and slipping into the car that was waiting for her in the driveway. She had been out for two consecutive nights; she must have come back just before dawn, before Grandma woke up. He would have taken me with him if he had known that Grandma was more distracted but also more afraid than ever before, and that was what made her so unyielding. My knees burned, and sometimes the skin peeled off, but Grandma was pleased. She would kiss my head or my forehead, then fall asleep, and I would tell myself that it was enough, enough to save me, even if I stayed there.

•

IT HAPPENED AT night, while we were asleep. It happened at night, and when we woke up we did not understand. My mother went in first, then me. There was some morning light inside, coming from the corridor rather than the window, illuminating the wooden dressing table where my grandma kept her family portraits, mementos of the dead, prayer cards, and the little jewelry she possessed, all laid out over a lace doily. Grandma lay still, her arms crossed over her chest as if she had already been readied for burial.

TEN

THE NIGHT OF THE FUNERAL, MY MOTHER TUCKED
me into bed. Her makeup was smudged and her eyes were
puffy, but she seemed incredibly beautiful to me. That may
have been the first time I ever truly understood how other people must see her.

"We'll have to get used to being alone," she told me.

We had buried Grandma in the town cemetery, next to my
grandfather. I knew the place; Grandma used to go there every

week, and occasionally she would take me with her. We would
pick flowers from the garden and put them on his headstone,
throw away the ones that had withered from the week before,
change their water when it got murky. Now my mother and I
would have to do the same.

My mother had picked one of her own dresses out for
Grandma, as she didn't think Grandma had any pretty ones
of her own—only ones she used to wear to work on the farm
or to go to church, back when she still used to. They were
all gray, and they all looked the same. So my mother put her
in a blue dress she said reminded her of the color of Grandma's eyes; they were closed now, and we would be able to see
them only if we pictured them in our minds. The dress suited
Grandma; they were the same height, both of them slender.

There were twenty-five people at the funeral. A few old
ladies from town, from among those friends who still remembered her; Enzo, who looked like he had been crying until a
minute ago and kept shaking his head as he stared at the hole
in the ground waiting to be filled; my aunts and their families,
Grandma's sisters, Uncle Michele. I looked at him; he returned
my look and waved. He hardly even knew me. I watched him
walk up to the gravestone after Grandma had already been
put in the ground, after everyone else had left.

My father had returned from Russia; that had made me
happy. He had come especially to bid farewell to Grandma.
I thought that for once she would have been proud of him.
My paternal grandparents were there, too. They kept looking
at me, kept saying, You've grown so much. But I didn't want
them to look at me. It was Grandma's day.

Stefano also came. He hugged me and told me, Take care of your mother—she'll need it now. He stood to one side, observing from a distance. I watched him hug my mother too, then leave before everyone else did.

Ilaria had come with her parents, who spoke to me kindly and held me close, even though they knew that Ilaria and I had argued, even though I could tell from the look in their eyes that she had told them everything, that they detested me for having caused their daughter pain. Ilaria didn't talk to me, nor did she approach me, though she looked at me for a long time, and for a moment I hoped she might come over. I would have gone to her myself, I would have liked to, but instead I walked out of the church to look at the fields and at the bleak church square in the morning, and to think of Grandma, without being able to cry.

My period had come back. I was a woman through and through.

Grandma's coffin was sealed for the burial, and my mother wasn't there when they lowered it into the ground. She didn't want to see. During the twenty minutes it took, she disappeared, and no one went to look for her. Not my father, not me; perhaps I should have, but I could not take my eyes off the ropes that were lowering my grandma into the belly of the earth. They put her next to my grandfather. I looked at his gravestone, which I had seen only a few times before, marked with a date so close to my birthday that it gave me pause every time. Now Grandma would lie beside him and I would remember her dates in the same way, carved into marble, the only part of her I could still touch.

•

MY FATHER WAS staying with his parents. I wished I could have done that too—gone with him, stayed with him. Now that Grandma was gone, everything felt different. It was quieter, even though Grandma hadn't talked very much, but now the sound of her huffing was gone, of her firm footsteps on the living room parquet or on the cold kitchen floor; the sight of her moving among the trees and in the orchard, scolding the farm hands for tasks they hadn't finished or had bungled somehow, and ending up completing them herself. The sound of chatter when she and my mother would sit confabulating in the dining room, their voices filtering through like gravel crunched underfoot, like rainfall, and every time I heard it I would assume they must be talking about me.

I wished I could go with my father, to stay with him in a house I hardly knew, a house I'd been to only a few times, for lunch or dinner, and that had always felt like it was made of marble, untouchable. Anything would have been better than this place that had been left hollowed out, like in the aftermath of a raid or a fire.

•

MY MOTHER TUCKED me into bed that night, then closed her eyes and turned her face away. I thought she must be crying again; I squeezed her arm and moved closer.

She shook her head, opened her eyes wide, and sniffed.

She had managed not to shed a single tear. "It won't be too bad, you'll see. We have a whole new life ahead of us now. We can do what we want with it."

"Whatever we want?" I said.

She shifted toward me, leaning close. Underneath the scent of toothpaste, her breath smelled of alcohol and cigarette smoke. I had never smelled that on her before. Only on Grandma, when she sat on the porch in the evenings drinking Enzo's wine and smoking one of her thin cigarettes.

"We can move to a different house. To a different city. I can find a new job, a new school for you. It's not so hard to start over. It's easier when you do it from scratch."

She stroked my hair. Her hands were cold.

I thought that Grandma would not be pleased to hear this, that she was bound to be angry. The dead see everything, I thought. The dead see everything.

"I still remember what it was like to be your age. I remember it like it was yesterday," she said, smiling in that way of hers—with just one side of her mouth, as if a piece of invisible string were pulling at its corner.

"I wouldn't have wanted it to be this way," she said. "I had other plans. For me, for us both. I wouldn't have wanted to leave you with all of this."

"I like it here," I said.

"But wouldn't you want to go somewhere else?"

"I think so," I replied. "Yes. I'd like that. But I like it here, too."

She sighed. "You'll understand when you're older. This place," she said, "this place is like dust. It doesn't matter how hard you try to get rid of it. It always comes back, and then you have to start all over again."

She took my hands and clasped them in hers as if to warm them up, though hers were colder.

"I don't want to leave you with this, Valentina. I don't want to leave you with this castle, this empire of dirt. This may be where we were born, but we don't have to stay here. Neither you nor I are made for this, that much I'm sure of. And now I think the time has come. Do you remember that song? I used to listen to it all the time, and you loved it, too. I think we've got to find our destiny, find our destiny before it gets too late."

She stroked my hair again. Her hands were tepid now. I realized I was feeling cold, and wondered if my own warmth had transferred into her.

"You're growing up now," she said. "But we were both children, you know? I was a child when I had you. In those first few days, in those first few months, every time I held you, every time you cried and I didn't know how to make you stop, I would pretend you were my little sister. Not my daughter, but some other child that fate had chosen to bring into this house. After all, Grandma could still have had more children of her own if she'd wanted to. I really did believe it, and after a while, you'd calm down, as if you could feel it, too. But I stopped thinking that way eventually. You were mine, you'd come out of me, and I wasn't going to trade that for the world."

Afterward she tucked me in the way she used to do when I was very, very little, back when she made sure to do it before and after my father, before and after my grandmother, so that it was always her idea first, so that she would be the last thing, the very last thing my eyes saw before they closed for the night.

●

MY FATHER AND my mother had a talk. They did it in the living room in the evening after everyone else had left and the house had gone back to the way I knew it: empty, large, and silent, a box soundproofed against the noise of the outside world, as if it were floating in the air high enough to be left undisturbed. I eavesdropped on their conversation from one of the rooms next door, sitting on the floor the way I used to do when my mother and my grandmother had one of their talks. They were talking about themselves, and they were talking about me. It wasn't anything I wasn't supposed to hear; maybe they knew I was there, and maybe they didn't care. My mother said: I wasn't expecting it. It all happened so fast. I stop to think for a moment and I'm thirty years old, and one day I feel like I've still got my whole life ahead of me, and the next day I feel like I've already died. You're always exaggerating, my father replied. You used to like it, though—this was her again—you used to *love* that about me. I still do. But it's not easy to deal with it every day. You dealt with it for years, she replied. He was silent for a while. I would have continued to do so. You know I would have wanted to. Every now and then I wake up in the middle of the night and I feel as if I'm still here, as if you're next to me, and when I open my eyes, and focus, and realize that's not the case, I feel something inside my chest, as if it's crawling with insects. But there's not even a sliver of a place for me here now.

•

I SLEPT VERY little that night. I didn't dream of anything in particular, but I kept waking up. The first thing I saw in the morning was the crack in the wall. It wasn't bleeding; it was just there, unmoving, like a carving, like something that had come into being with the house itself, that had remained there, watching, since time immemorial. If I concentrated hard enough, I could make myself remember the blur of the blood, red at first, then purple, then green—like a bruise, like a trail of mold.

It was Sunday, and the town's church bells were ringing. Grandma would have begun praying now, silent and alone in her room; it was her against the world, inside that little temple she had built to furiously pray to her god, who had listened to her and obliged her right until the end. The house was quieter during that hour; it always had been. I could hear even the slightest of sounds—of wood creaking, of the wind sighing through half-open doors—like those of a body shifting in its sleep.

I was staring at the crack that evening when my mother walked in. I didn't even notice that she was there until she sat down on the bed.

"Have you ever lied to me, Valentina?"

I started. I stalled: "What do you mean?"

"You know what I mean. I asked you if you've ever lied to me."

I didn't say anything. I felt my heart beating; I could hear it. It was making an incredible amount of noise.

"We all tell lies, Valentina. And then we cover them up. We spend our whole lives hiding them, and we might even manage to forget them for a while. But they grow there, underground where they've been put, until they become enormous. Until they come for us. Sooner or later, they always come for us."

She was talking like Grandma used to. That was the feeling I had, I remember it clearly: she was talking like Grandma. I had never noticed how similar their voices sounded.

"I haven't told you any lies," I said.

"I have. They're not lies, they're things I've hidden from you. Secrets. I put them inside a box and I buried them. But Grandma always used to say that choosing not to tell is just the same as lying, remember? I never believed her then, but I think it must be true. Secrets never forget about you either, just like lies."

She looked up, her gaze fixed on the crack in the wall. "It's all about to come crashing down," she said. She laughed in the way she always did. There was no trace of Grandma in that laugh. That much I was absolutely sure of. "It's getting bigger, isn't it? It's my fault."

"No," I said. "It was me."

"Now that Grandma's no longer here, the whole house will go with her."

I hated her when she behaved like this. That was when I first became aware of it: I hated her and I hated Grandma, how they turned every event into something so theatrical, so dramatic. Their way of treating every act as if it were a cog in a much larger wheel, of soaking everything in tension, like an overexposed photograph, the way they left you with no way out, and ultimately ensured that our fates were already written.

Aren't you happy? I wanted to ask her, though I didn't. Isn't this what you always wanted?

"Do you think Grandma loved me?" she asked.

"Yes," I replied.

"That's not true," she laughed. "You don't really believe that."

I demurred. I hated when she cornered me like this, just for the fun of it.

"But you're right. It's true. She wasn't exactly proud of me, but she did love me. Maybe more than she loved your aunts—at least that's what they always said." She smiled. "It's something I was never able to prevent."

She stood up. Slowly, as if she were performing a choreography. Her hair, messy and electric, crowned her face, sending radiation all around it. She went to the window and looked out, then turned toward me again.

"I never asked to be loved. When I was little, all I wanted was to disappear. But instead there was your grandmother, your grandfather, first your aunts and then your father, and then you as well. Your father once told me he had fallen in love with me because of my light. He told me that there was a peculiar, powerful light somewhere inside me, and that this light is what made him fall in love with me. But I don't think that's the case. Human beings are not like other animals, not like plants. We're not attracted to light, but to darkness. We are drawn to that which we cannot understand, to what scares us. We fall in love with filth, with dirt, with snags more than we do with perfection. And I believe it's this, this thing I have inside me, this curse I carry, that keeps you all so close to me."

She stopped to breathe for a moment, swallowed, looked outside. She was staring into space; there was nothing to look at, out there. Just darkness.

"Did you know that you could have had siblings?"

"What?"

"Would you have liked that?"

I thought about it. A long time ago, maybe. But not anymore. "I don't know," I replied.

"You used to always ask me about it when you were little."

"I wouldn't like it now. I'm used to this. And I'd be too grown up for it anyway. I'm too grown up now."

"You could have had them," she said. "Two of them, two boys. One would be nine by now. The other would have been due five months from now."

I felt something inside me, like a cold lump. I felt it in my chest, and later in my stomach. "What does that mean?"

"Do you know what an abortion is?" she asked. She blasted air out of her mouth, and the hard gust of it sounded like laughter. "You do, of course you do, you're old enough. What it means is that I've had two abortions. The first time wasn't my choice; he left on his own, in the middle of the night. One day he was inside me, the next day he was gone. He was small, he was tiny, I hadn't told anyone about him yet. But I could feel that he was a boy."

She scratched her nose, as if to check that it was still there.

She seemed to have no expression at all. It was as if she was acting a part. "The second time was my decision."

I looked at her for a long time, at that face everyone said was so beautiful, and that must have made my father fall in love with her all that time ago. I started to cry. I wanted to hold it back, but I couldn't. "Why?" I asked.

"It was a boy," she said. "It went the way it was supposed to go."

My heart was beating tremendously hard. It felt like it would break out, crack my chest open and break out. I don't think I had ever been so angry at anyone before. I sat there on the bed and shook. Later I would learn—I don't recall where or from whom—that our bodies shake when there is something we want to do but we prevent ourselves from doing it. That tremor is the ghost of our desire, moving beyond us, beyond the body, and coming to fruition. Embracing, attacking, and fleeing.

My mother was looking at me, trying to console me. "I hoped it would end everything. I thought I would do it for Grandma."

"Why?" I asked once more.

"Because I knew it was my fault. Everything that's happened here, everything that's happened these past few months, it's all my fault."

"That's not true," I said. I repeated those words, again and again, but only in my head.

"I'm afraid it is. I haven't been a good person, a good daughter. I haven't even been a good mother."

She waited. Her eyes were red and wide. "I hoped it would save her. We all hoped to save her, didn't we? We all tried."

"Does Dad know?"

"No," she replied. "Can I trust you?"

She waited until she saw me nodding. "I'm the only one who noticed, and I didn't tell him. I told him to leave before I had even decided what to do about it."

"Why?"

"It had nothing to do with him anymore. The choice was mine, it had to be mine alone. He was inside here," she said, touching her abdomen. "I asked him to leave and he did. I didn't want him to. It was stupid. But it's too late for excuses."

"What about Grandma?" I asked. My voice was nearly gone now. "Did she know?"

"I think she figured it out," she said. "I've never managed to hide anything from her for very long."

Her hand was still resting on her stomach. She lifted it and placed it over my cheek.

"I wanted you to be the only one, Valentina. Just you and me. Everyone else comes and goes, they're only good for keeping us going, but what really counts is you and me. And Grandma, wherever she is."

•

IT WAS A while before I stopped shaking. I could feel the shivers all the way under my skin, in my teeth, as if they might fall out at any moment. After I stopped shaking, I ran away. Not right then and there, but later, while she slept. I don't recall how, the precise method and moment of my exit from that house—my house—that night. It's strange: I remember absences more than I remember actions. I remember the house at night as I walked away, how it looked smaller—as it always did at nighttime—how it got smaller and smaller as my feet, my twelve-year-old's legs (if I concentrate I can still feel the sensation of my thighs rubbing against each other, their touch—so repulsive to me—a constant reminder that I was growing), took me down the street that led to town. I remember an earlier moment too, a detail: the locusts were still there, on the walls. They'd never left. Small, fleet-legged insects, stepping all over the stone walls as if to claim their territory. The house is yours, I thought to myself. The house is yours now. I wanted to shout it out. Perhaps I did.

I had to decide where to go. There were two people I could think of, but I would have been embarrassed to show up at Marco's at that time of night; I would have had to come up with some excuse, especially for his mother. As for Ilaria, I was afraid of the way she might look at me, and of her silence, all of it so different from what I had always known her for. I walked quickly; I was cold. We had gone down this road dozens of times over the summer: it was where we had met Marco; it was the route we had always taken to visit each other's homes over the years. I didn't even know what time it was, but it must have been just after dinner. In the distance, the lights of other people's houses were on: as I walked farther and farther, I counted those I could see, fixating on their amber reflections on the fields as if they could somehow bring me warmth. I passed in front of Marco's house and stopped in the front yard, staring at the lights and waiting to see if I could recognize anyone's shadow behind the windows. I didn't see anyone. So I kept going all the way to town, counting my steps just to have something to do, and wondering if Grandma had ever done the same in all the years she had walked along that road.

When I got to Ilaria's, they had already eaten. They were very concerned when I turned up, and wondered if something had happened to my mother. They made me sit down. They asked me many questions. I told them it was not good for me to be in that house, the house where Grandma had died. They said: Your mother must be hurting, too. You should be there for her. I told them that she had agreed to this, that she wanted to be left alone for a little while, that she was crying a lot and didn't want me to see her that way. I told them that she didn't want me to stay in that place. I said all this with her words in my mind. Eventually they agreed to let me spend the night there so long as I called my mother first. I didn't want to speak to her, so I made them call. They gave me the guest bedroom, where the bed had just been made with fresh sheets that smelled good. Ilaria came to the door to wish me good night. It's incredible what people will forgive when the end comes close.

THE LAND VOMITS OUT ITS INHABITANTS

I WOULD HAVE LIKED TO HAVE A BROTHER. I CAN
see that now that the years have passed. I would have liked to
have a brother. But it's more than that: it's the sense of an existence, a presence, like a phantom limb. I have never stopped
believing these things: the way you are raised defines who you
are. It doesn't matter how many years you waste trying to convince yourself of the opposite, how much money you spend
on therapy, travel, clothes. The men you recruit to reassure

or admire you, all your condescending girlfriends. The place where you were born is something you carry inside you, underneath your skin, no matter how much time you spend striving to get it out.

The day my mother had her abortion I was in the room next door. She confessed it to me herself, much later. I was right there and I didn't hear her screaming or whimpering or anything of that sort. The blood poured out of her as it had out of me for the first time that night, signaling that her womb was empty again, and ready for a new life, should she want another. The blood was an ending or a beginning. We both knew that.

Her body would not relent. That was her burden, the cruelty of it all: body and mind at odds. In nature's eyes she was a mother, and she always would be: sterile and fecund at once.

•

OUR GUILT POURED out with the blood. We realized without needing to put it into words that we could forgive ourselves. Now that Grandma was no longer with us, we managed to convince ourselves—silently, each on her own, sharing only a space, a corner of the couch at night before we went to sleep, a hug—that none of what had happened had anything to do with us. Gradually we began to see everything more clearly, and the memories of that summer seemed to turn blurry, as if they were behind a dirty glass. All we were left with were sensations that eventually faded into a sort of itch, a numbness, like in the aftermath of an illness or a bout of fever.

There was gossip in town still, but we had learned not to hear it.

·

MY FATHER CAME back. He changed jobs, tired of traveling. He was hired by a company that manufactured cups a hundred kilometers from where we were. I went to visit him sometimes; I would spend the night there and he would take me to see the factory. He would show me how the glass was molded. He never touched any of it—he was higher up; he had an office and a desk, where he'd put a photo of me as a five-year-old. He'd made a career for himself, as they say. My mother watched his progress with admiration and anguish, like something that she'd let slip from her grasp but that she was too proud to ever take back, something she had pushed away little by little at first then right off, making a clean cut, without ever even realizing what she was doing, or maybe as an act of aimless defiance, her against the world. He had learned to forgive her, but he would not go back to her. He still saw her as the girl from the woods, someone he could never truly understand, but now he was tired of looking for her. Neither of them saw the other as they had when they had first met, at sixteen, nor as they had seen each other later, when my mother had confessed to him that she was pregnant with me.

   That's how I pictured them, my mother and father. Full of illusions and resignation as they stood before furniture shop windows and imagined themselves in homes they would never have, the oak dining table, the lacquered kitchen cabinets, the floor—not too light or it would get dirty straightaway, not too dark or the dust would stand out—the bedroom, the bathroom. Standing there for hours before coming back down to earth, back to the place she would never leave behind, her stone tower without stairs. The leash on her was short and woven with guilt.

Now she was the one looking at him from somewhere else. She looked at him and she saw the missed chances, the chasms, the parallel universes. He returned her gaze from a cosmic distance. Time had devoured them both.

But I didn't. I stayed with her, because I was twelve years old and had nowhere else to go. I was not given a choice, and even if I had been, I could not have done otherwise. When I went back the day after I ran away, I found her in tears. She drew me to her and made me promise I would never do it again. She told me she had chosen to have me and that she would never allow anything or anyone to take me away. I believed her, because I could see how fragile she was without me, how little of her there was, and that was enough for me. I realized this not in the moment, but later on; you cannot really understand when you're twelve, when your reality is cushioned, inhabited by what you've been told and what you think you know. So you act instinctively—but that impulse holds within it the germ of truth, the thing that will define who you are when you are finally capable of recognizing it.

We stayed, my mother and I, to watch what was left gradually crumble around us. We stayed, simply because there was nothing else to do. My mother was no longer the girl from the woods; that part of her had been left behind somewhere, in some clearing in the middle of the night. Grandma had taught her how to stay. She had taught her resignation, solidity, forbearance, pride. And microscopic vengeance, which was necessary to keep going, and almost entirely invisible to those who do not practice it themselves, who do not know how: a word of bad advice, a lie disguised as truth, a sudden, cutting remark. Grandma had taught her in her own way, never speaking of it but passing it all on discreetly: a silent inheritance somewhere in the genes, unfurling in its own time. Somewhere inside, that inheritance had grown and developed. Those who did not know my mother well would not have noticed the difference. She's the same as ever, they would have said, only a little older, scalded and hardened by time and by the world. But only just; she still twirled her hair, still let out her laugh. She was good at it.

We stayed for another five years, still and watchful, my mother doing nothing at all to save a house that was now doomed, terminal, and instead planning her departure, cajoling me, singing her song, thinking of the how and the where even as the when seemed both near and incredibly far. We saw the cracks in the walls grow larger, furrows like wrinkles that crawled down from the corners of the walls as if to catch us, to grab us. Anyone who walked past could see it; everyone kept saying that one of these days the house was going to collapse onto our heads. They said it was cursed, infested; they counted the insects on the blind walls and remembered the time when someone walking down the road had seen those walls become covered in black, in thousands and thousands of locusts, swarming and seething like ants over a carcass, the color of dried blood.

Nobody wanted to buy our produce anymore, but it didn't matter, because my mother sold off the livestock and let the vegetable garden rot and the soil dry out.

It took five years for her to keep her promise that we would go away, that she would take us away. Five years and a crack that was bigger than the others, a crack that opened up one day, expanded silently, and broke the roof in half one summer.

We walked out of there as two women. We moved away, we separated. I did what she had not been able to do: I went to university, I chose a bigger city. I rented a home with another young woman, an apartment in an industrial district, two rooms, large windows, and no curtains. During the winter I would stare out at the factories, the thick smoke coming out of their chimneys, the red brick and the gray sheet metal against the white sky. My mother stayed in another town. She picked a place in the center, bigger than mine, where she stored everything we had taken with us. We were still young, we had our lives ahead of us. We blended into the world.